MW01600876

THE

DELIVERS

by

Paula F. Winskye

I

"Tony," Sheriff Ryan Clark's voice crackled over the radio. "You anywhere near the Fisher place?"

Law Enforcement Ranger Tony Wagner keyed his mike. "Real close as the crow flies, but about five miles by road."

"Can you meet me over there?"

"Yeah. See you in a few."

Tony made a u-turn on the deserted Evergreen National Park road with a feeling of foreboding. Peaceful Benson County, Colorado rarely needed him for another of his jobs—deputy detective. The courses he had taken for his third job—FBI consultant—made him the most qualified investigator in the county.

Ryan tried not to interfere with his full-time National Park Service job. He only called Tony for major crimes.

Tony knew everyone in the vicinity of the park. The Fishers even attended the same church. Though, between their busy lives and his work schedule, he probably only talked to them once a month. They were not friends in the "come for dinner" sense, but their shared faith provided a stronger bond.

He pulled the park service pickup to the shoulder of the gravel road near the Fisher's overflowing mailbox and waited. An acre of spruce and pine hid the house. Two sets of tire tracks discolored the late spring snow that had fallen the night before. *Probably the same vehicle, coming and going.*

Ryan stopped beside him and lowered his window. "Vince says their mail hasn't been picked up since Saturday. He figured they were gone, but when he took a registered letter up to the house today, the car and pickup are both there."

Tony ran his hand through his blond hair. "How you want to do this?"

"Treat it as a crime scene until proven otherwise."

Tony pulled on his park service baseball cap and climbed from his pickup. "Preserve the evidence. I'll ride with you so we don't track up the yard any more than we have to."

Ryan stayed on the shoulder of the driveway, stopping just inside the trees, still a hundred feet from the two-story house. Nothing stirred.

Tony scanned the yard. "Where's their dog?"

Ryan stroked his bushy mustache, his jaw clenched. "Go around back. Try the door."

"Did Vince?"

"No. He got spooked."

"I don't blame him."

Tony pulled his .45 and jogged around the house, using the cover of trees that dotted the yard. At six feet, two inches, with a body hardened by cross country skiing, he neared the back door before Ryan reached the porch. He heard Ryan knock on the front door and call Blake and Jill Fisher's names.

After looking through windows into an empty kitchen and laundry room, he did the same. He turned the knob and entered a mud room. Four sets of winter boots—one large, three smaller—sat beneath hooks full of winter coats and sweatshirts.

He stood beside the door and nudged it open, surveying the kitchen before entering. Breakfast dishes littered the table, as if the family had just gone to the next room. A carton of milk sat open on the counter. He felt it with the back of his hand. Room temperature. He smelled it and jerked back.

"Sour."

"Tony, you found anything?"

"Somebody left in a hurry."

"M-m. I found a broken coffee cup and dried coffee by the front door. Let's stick together. Don't know what we'll find."

"Gloves."

Ryan nodded and they donned disposable gloves before searching an office and master bedroom downstairs and three bedrooms upstairs. They found no sign of the Fishers or their two teenaged daughters and no clue to their whereabouts.

Tony sighed. "I can't think of any way this can have a good ending."

"No." Ryan rubbed his mustache again. "This place doesn't have a basement. We'd better take a look through the outbuildings."

"They have horses. If they were hungry, they'd have whinnied at us."

"Meaning?"

"I don't know. I'll see when I get to the barn." They searched the farm shop before moving to the barn. Four horses watched them with curiosity, but no hunger. A foot of hay remained in the bottom of a bale feeder. Tony studied the bales lined up outside the fence. "It'd take four horses five or six days to eat a bale that size."

"Fits Vince's time line."

They checked each stall in the hip roof barn, then surveyed a ladder into the hay mow. Ryan pointed to another ladder and used hand signals to indicate that they would both ascend at the same time. The two square foot openings would make the perfect spot for an ambush.

But once again, they found nothing. They climbed down and Ryan dusted off his clothes.

"One more building. Then we'd better call in the troops."

They walked with their guns lowered to the pole building, covered with corrugated tin at the edge of the trees. Ryan stepped through the door and stopped so suddenly that Tony nearly ran into him.

After the initial shock, Tony had to fight to keep his breakfast down. He had seen a hiker after a bear had fed on him, but nothing could prepare him for this.

Ryan, a combat veteran, needed to get away from the carnage. He leaned against the outside of the building.

"Sorry. I know we have to go in and see if Jill and the kids are there too. But I need a minute."

Tony nodded. "I'll go in. The killer's long gone. Take your time."

Tony fingered the cross around his neck and said a prayer before approaching Blake Fisher's body. He had been tied to one of the poles supporting the building, with duct tape over his mouth. He had been stabbed below the ribs, just a little left of center. Tony pulled his eyes away from the dried blood and noticed the bruising under the ropes. Blake had struggled for some time before he was killed.

In slow motion, Tony surveyed the building. Protruding from behind a baler, he saw socks and bare legs. He edged around the implement. Jill Fisher. Naked. Stabbed in the same location. Duct tape on her mouth and wrists. Her clothes strewn about.

"Here's Jill."

Ryan joined him. "Where are the girls?"

Tony shook his head. "There's no time to waste."

"I'll call the CBI. We don't know if the killers drove in, so use your tracking skills. I'll take care of everything else till reenforcements get here."

Tony nodded, relieved to get away from the gruesome scene in the building. He walked the edge of the clearing, making a mental note to repeat the process in a few hours, after the snow melted. Three-quarters of the way around the yard, he found the Fisher's German Shepherd. It had been stabbed. He sighed, then completed his circuit.

He followed Ryan's tracks to the pole building, but stayed outside. "I found the dog. I don't think the killers drove here. I think the dog found them hiding in the trees. Might find some DNA evidence in his teeth."

"I hope he took a chunk out of one of the bastards."

"Yeah. After the snow melts, I'll look around again. Any evidence will be under the snow."

"Good. I sent one of the deputies to the school to see when the girls attended last. You didn't see Fishers in church Sunday?"

"I had to work."

"Ask somebody about that. We're guessing Saturday, but until we get a coroner's report, that's all it is. We need to get a search started."

"I know, but not right now. We don't need a hundred volunteers running all over the mountains before I get a chance to look for tracks."

"Yeah. Yeah. You're their best chance, Tony. You stand a better chance of finding them than any hundred volunteers."

II

Tony checked for cell phone service and called the ranger station, rather than use the radio. Too many scanners. His wife, Kelly, answered. She had checked caller ID.

"Is it bad?"

"Couldn't be much worse. I need to talk to Don."

She put him on hold. In a moment he heard the hollow sound of Don's speaker phone.

"Kelly, close the door. Okay, Reverend, it's just Kelly and me here. What can you tell us?"

"It's bad. Blake and Jill Fisher have been murdered. Christi and Terri are missing."

"Lord. We won't expect you here for a while."

"And I don't suppose you'll be home soon," Kelly said.

"If I'm lucky, I'll get home for some sleep, but don't count on it. Just wanted you to know."

"Be careful."

"I'll do my best. Gotta go."

For the rest of the day, while the Colorado Bureau of Investigation collected evidence, Tony made ever-widening semi-circles around the farm yard, starting at the road and working his way back to it.

A quarter-mile from the house, on a path behind the building where he and Ryan had discovered the bodies, he found a tissue. He marked the spot, photographed it, then collected it in an evidence bag.

He did not change course, knowing the tissue could have been there days before the Fishers were killed. His neck ached from keeping his eyes on the ground. When he reached the path during the next circle, he stopped to rub it.

A faint movement caught his eye. When he tried to focus, he saw nothing. He advanced, keeping his eyes forward. Finally, he saw it, caught in the bark of a pine tree, about shoulder level. A long, blonde hair. He snapped a picture, left a marker, collected the hair, then radioed Ryan.

"Find something?"

"No tracks, so far. But I think I've found the route they took."

"Where you at?"

"You'll find a path behind the pole barn. A deer trail really. I'm maybe three-eighths of a mile west of there."

"I'll bring one of the CBI guys."

"10-4."

Tony walked up the trail, looking for tracks while he waited. When he heard them coming, he returned. Warren, the CBI agent looked like a former linebacker.

"What'd you find?"

"You saw my first marker?" The agent nodded and Tony held up the tissue. He waved toward his second marker and showed the hair in the evidence bag. "I found this about shoulder level. The younger girl is blond and maybe five, four."

"Not much. Those girls probably spent a lot of time out here."

"True. But it's worth following up."

"Go ahead. We have an unidentified set of tire tracks. Tell us if you find any solid leads. You coming, sheriff?"

"In a while." Ryan waited for him to leave. "What do you think, Tony?"

"I don't know. It's not much. We know the killers came in the morning. The ground would have been frozen. No tracks. Instead of working back and forth, I'm going to stay on this trail for a while."

"Need me for anything?"

"I don't think I'll find 'em before dark, so I should be fine on my own."

"You had anything to eat?"

"No."

Ryan pulled a candy bar from his coat pocket. "Best I can do right now."

"I'll take chocolate over a steak any day."

***

Tony had spent every spare moment of his childhood in the woods around his Wisconsin home, fascinated by the animals, teaching himself to read signs. Twelve years in Evergreen National Park had made him just as familiar with the Colorado mountains. He felt far more useful and comfortable out here than collecting evidence at the crime scene.

The FBI kept him on retainer for just such cases. They had hauled him to several states where either his tracking or rock climbing skills would benefit the case. They had once called him as an expert witness. That part of the job he could live without.

He unzipped his coat and considered leaving it. He would return this way when darkness approached. Instead, he slipped it off his right arm, out of the way of his gun. The weather could change quickly at this time of year.

Each time another deer trail forked off the more used one, he scouted it, searching for broken branches that would indicate if something taller than a deer had passed. Each time he returned to the main trail.

The elevation had risen steadily behind the Fisher place. Finally, he reached a bare ridge and surveyed the land beyond. He felt a sense of hopelessness. Nothing but mountains for thirty or forty miles. *I don't even know if I'm on the right trail.*

Maybe the CBI has the right idea. The killers had driven into the yard and left the same way. Tony shook his head. Everything he had seen told him otherwise.

"Lord, you've given me a tough problem. You know I can't do this without your help. Give me the skills I need to find those girls."

He scanned the sky. Dark clouds shrouded the mountains to the northwest. The sun hung low over the western horizon. *Should I start back? In a little while.* He descended the other side of the ridge. Within a few yards forest surrounded him again. As he had done all day, every few feet he looked up from the trail, surveying his surroundings.

This time, he spotted it right away. Hair. Short. Black. Course. Probably black bear. But this, too, he found about shoulder level. A bear scratching his back on a tree or climbing might leave it that high. But either of those activities would have dislodged bark from the tree. The bark remained undisturbed.

Tony marked, photographed, and collected the hair, then backtracked. As he reached the ridge, a cold wind gust pushed him forward. He pulled on his coat and surveyed the cloud bank, now threatening to blot out the setting sun. He hurried toward the Fisher ranch.

***

"Tony, you copy." Ryan's voice sounded worried.

"Yeah. I'm coming. It'll probably be another half-hour."

"You can't track in the dark."

"It wasn't dark when I quit tracking."

"Anything?"

"Nothing definite. Let me quit talking so I can watch where I'm putting my feet."

Ryan chuckled. "See you when you get here."

Tony's flashlight illuminated the path. But watching where he put his feet sometimes kept him from seeing the branch about to hit his face. Even in the dark, his own tracks were easy to follow until he reached the point where he had been walking on frozen ground. From there, when the trees thinned enough to make the sky visible, he could see the glow of the ranch lights ahead.

Reaching his first marker, he noticed that the light produced came from more than a couple of mercury vapor yard lights. Evidently the CBI had set up extra lighting.

"Working late. I thought they'd have been done by now."

When he walked out of the trees, a small woman in a CBI coat, standing near the pole barn, shrieked.

"Sorry, ma'am. Ranger Tony Wagner."

"Oh. What are you doing here?"

"Special Deputy."

"Oh."

"Have you seen the sheriff?"

"Check in front of the house."

"Thanks." He found Ryan standing beside a motor home, drinking coffee. He poured a cup for Tony. "Thanks."

"You look beat."

"No kidding."

Warren came from the motor home. "Anything."

Tony retrieved the evidence bag from his pocket. "Probably black bear, but I don't think a black bear left it."

"Huh?"

"A black bear, losing hair on the trunk of a tree this high." He held his hand at shoulder level. "Would have left some other signs. I think this came from some kind of coat."

"That's a reach."

"Like one set of tire tracks that might have been left by a hundred local people, including the mailman who called this in?"

Warren glared. "We'll have the lab analyze it. See if they find anything unusual. The sheriff's been waiting for you so he can leave. Go back to town and write your reports."

"Waiting? I have my own vehicle."

Ryan nodded toward the road. "I told Don to come get it. Wouldn't want the Park Service to protest about you using their pickup on county business."

"M-m. Good. I didn't feel like driving anyhow."

III

By the time Tony finished his report, eating supper in the process, and Ryan dropped him off at his Park Service house, his watch read 11:30. He switched on the kitchen light and sat down to unlace his boots. Kelly came from their bedroom.

"Love you."

He smiled. "I love you. Did I wake you?"

"Yeah. I figured I could at least catch a cat nap before you got home. I never know how late it'll be." He stood and they hugged. "Do they have any idea where the girls are?"

"No."

"It's all over town already. They had a prayer service at church this evening. Everybody asked about you. I told them you were working on it. That seemed to make them feel better."

He sighed and smoothed her short, brown hair, messed up from sleep. "I don't know if I can do anything this time."

"You can do what the Lord wants you to do. Pastor Johnson prayed that God would grant you and all the investigators the skills you needed to find the girls."

He nodded. "How are the kids?"

"Justin's fine. Christina doesn't really understand. But Brett's kind of worried."

"I'll talk to him in the morning."

"I'll bet you just want to fall into bed."

"After a shower."

"But that'll wake you up."

He gave her a long, wet kiss. "I know."

"You need to unwind."

"I *really* need to unwind."

"I'll be waiting for you."

***

After some very intense lovemaking, Tony and Kelly passed out in each other's arms.

At 4:30 AM, Tony woke to the sound of someone pounding on the kitchen door. He dragged himself to a sitting position as they pounded again.

"I'm coming," he mumbled.

"Who's that?"

"It's for me. Go back to sleep."

"Kay."

He heaved himself to his feet, fumbled for his robe, and shuffled to the hall. After closing the bedroom door, he pulled on the robe before turning on the hall light. The pounding stopped. He yawned and tied the robe on his way across the kitchen. He turned on the outside light and recognized the person with the black hair and bushy eyebrows on the other side of the door.

"Huh?" He opened the door.

"Morning, Tony," FBI agent Wyatt Garret said with barely a trace of a Texas drawl.

"Huh? You'll have to explain this one. Come in."

Tony flipped on the kitchen light and punched the button on the coffee maker before sinking into a chair.

Garret closed the door and joined him at the table, smiling. "You look like hell."

"You know what I saw yesterday. Then I spent all day hiking the mountains and all evening doing paperwork. And you wake me up after about four-and-a-half hours sleep. You'd look like heck too."

"I'm sure. So, you want to know how I got this case. I have enough seniority to have cases flagged for me. If your name shows up, I get a call."

Tony's chuckle turned into a yawn. "The guys who work for you must really hate me. You treat everyone else like dirt, but go out of your way to work with me."

"Hey. You're the Reverend. Even I can't chew out somebody with that title."

"Uh-huh. So you just drop everything and head to Spruce Lake?"

"I was on vacation."

"So your wife hates me."

"No. She was glad to get rid of me. I'd fixed about everything that needed fixing."

Tony heaved himself from the chair and poured coffee, adding milk to his.

"So what's our first move, boss?"

"You tell me."

The baby crying interrupted them. "Drink your coffee. I'll be right back."

He hurried to the room Justin shared with Christina. As soon as the baby heard his voice, he stopped crying. Tony changed his diaper and brought him to the kitchen. He made introductions while warming a bottle.

"This is Justin Donald. Justin, this ugly guy is Agent Garret. He arrested your daddy a long time ago."

Justin's chubby face scowled and Garret laughed. "Great first impression. You been having a lot of sleepless nights?"

"No. He's amazing. He's been sleeping all night for a couple months. He gets up about this time every morning, then naps till about seven. He's been a dream compared to Brett and Christina."

"You weren't even around when Brett was a baby."

Tony sat and offered Justin the bottle. "Kelly reminded me of that every time Christina woke us. I had to get up most of the time to make up for not being around. Although I pointed out that I didn't even know Brett existed until she showed up here when he was five. Now, where were we?"

"What's our first move?"

"Get some horses and get back on that trail."

"You don't think the tire tracks are significant?"

"No."

"Why not?"

"The dog." Garret waited for him to continue. He would tell Tony afterward if he disagreed. "The dog found somebody, who killed him. They didn't drive in. They walked in."

Garret nodded. "Even if we're wrong, there are plenty city-bred agents to follow up on the tire tracks. That trail is already old. We need to get on it."

"Anybody else going with us?"

"Not right now. Let's see if you can find any actual tracks."

"Guess you've read my report."

"Of course. Your boy's asleep. I suggest you do the same till seven. I'll go to the sheriff's office and arrange transportation for us and some horses."

"I'll take Chance. Wake up Neil White to bring a horse for you."

"Yeah. We've used him before. I'll meet you here at Park Headquarters at eight. Have Chance ready to load."

"Okay. Plan to stay out overnight."

Garret growled.

IV

Thick overcast delayed the onset of daylight. Tony and Garret discussed the trip on the drive to the Fisher place.

"We can't really follow most of that deer trail on horseback," Tony explained. "We'll take a more roundabout way to the ridge, but it'll be faster. Unless you want to see the trail."

Garret shook his head. "I doubt I'd find anything you didn't. Let's save all the time we can. Hope it doesn't snow."

Tony studied the sky. "You go ahead and hope. I'll pray. And I bet we'll get white anyhow."

Garret laughed. "A realist."

He pulled into the ranch yard, now occupied by only the motor home and one other law enforcement vehicle. Two men met them, their coats announcing them as FBI agents. He growled some orders while Tony unloaded horses. Within fifteen minutes they rode uphill.

Traveling at their smooth middle gait, the Tennessee Walking Horses reached the ridge in an hour and a half. Tony dismounted and patted Chance's sweat-soaked neck.

"We'll lead them from here. They need the break and it'll be easier for me to track."

They walked to the place where he had found the bear hair and he picked up where he had left off the previous day. The air smelled of snow and a cold, northwest wind chilled them any time they reached a clearing. An hour passed while they descended into a valley. Occasional snowflakes drifted from the clouds.

Tony again checked every trail that branched off from this one. Only deer and elk had left tracks here. Again he felt hopeless. If the trail forked into two well traveled paths, he would be groping. They might as well recruit a hundred volunteers and hope one of them stumbled upon some signs.

"Tony."

He looked up from the trail and saw Garret pointing at the trunk of a tree. Three feet off the ground, a denim thread fluttered in the breeze. Tony said a prayer of thanks, while Garret marked, photographed, and collected it.

"Thanks. I might have missed that."

"I've got your back."

A snow melt swollen creek at the bottom of the narrow valley provided water for the horses. Tony looked upstream and down.

"They'd have to be nuts to wade this creek. They would have had to stay on this side at least till they found a place to cross. We'll hobble the horses and break out some lunch. Then one of us can walk each way for about 15 minutes, see if we find anything. That'll give the horses time to graze."

Garret nodded. They left the horses in a meadow and Tony walked upstream, chewing on a piece of jerky. Before he had traveled a hundred yards, he froze. The patch of gravel at the stream's edge measured no more than three square feet. But there, obvious to even an amateur, lay the print of a hiking boot, probably a women's size 8.

"Garret!"

His voice echoed through the valley. Within a minute he saw the agent hurrying toward him. Tony crouched over the print and placed a marker beside it. When Garret saw it, he slapped him on the back.

"Reverend, you have God on your side. I was really starting to wonder if we'd ever find anything."

"So was I. Let's get the horses. We can ride for a while."

Garret snapped a picture before they returned to the horses. Tony led the way upstream. They found more footprints where a tree had fallen across the creek. He dismounted for a closer look.

"We have both girls, one in hiking boots and one in sneakers, and somebody wearing some kind of moccasins. Two. No. Probably three somebodies. You can see this log's been used as a bridge quite a few times. Let's go."

He urged Chance into the water, letting the sure-footed chestnut pick his way across the rocky bottom. The fast-rushing water nearly reached his belly. The gelding scrambled up the other bank, followed by Garret's black.

The girls now left an easy trail, traveling uphill and up the valley. Northwest. He and Garret rode, with Tony only dismounting occasionally for a closer look.

"Definitely three of them. Big guys. They leave a pretty deep track, even in moccasins."

"When we get to the top of this ridge, I'll call in. Report and give them a GPS fix on us. See if the lab has come up with anything useful."

***

Cold wind at the ridge top made them rethink that strategy. They backtracked to a more sheltered area, with grazing for the horses. Garret asked some questions before he called.

"Where are we headed? Are there any roads out this way?"

"No. We're headed into wilderness. Probably twenty miles before you even find a logging road. Might be a hunting cabin or two. We're on our own."

Garret made his call, his thick eyebrows nearly meeting. After reporting what he had found, he asked for forensic results. He listened with barely an interruption. If anything, his expression worsened.

"Okay. We'll discuss it and decide what to do." He disconnected. "There's a hell ... heck of a spring storm coming. Supposed to hit tomorrow night."

Tony frowned and dug a map out of his saddle bags. He spread it on a boulder and studied it for so long that Garret had to speak.

"What you looking for?"

"A way to keep going and survive."

"Oh." Garret let him study.

Finally Tony sighed. "It'll be risky."

"Tell me."

"If they keep going in this general direction and we don't find them, by noon tomorrow, we should be about here." He made a circle with his finger on the map. "We quit there and turn ninety degrees down this valley. We should be able to make it here before nightfall."

He indicated a tiny square on the map.

"What's that?"

"A building of some kind. Probably a cabin. The risk being that it may have burned down or fallen down since this map was made."

"You're just full of good news."

"The alternative is to start back in the morning."

"I'll follow you. Whatever you want to do."

"I want to find those girls. Let's go."

They mounted and got back on the trail. The tracks led across the ridge and into the next valley as Tony had hoped. Most of the time he could follow the trail on horseback. When it faded, usually a few minutes out of the saddle produced results. A slab of granite a hundred yards wide provided more of a challenge.

About mid-afternoon they came upon a campsite. Tony read the signs.

"They tied the girls to this tree. Close to the fire. They were pretty sure of themselves. Didn't think anyone could track them this far."

"They didn't know what a bulldog you are."

"When were Blake and Jill killed?"

"Coroner says probably Saturday."

"This fits. Let's go. We'll probably be without tracks for a while again. But it warmed up faster on Sunday. The ground would have thawed out earlier. Hopefully, they left other signs because they're over-confident. What else did that call tell you?"

"They got DNA from Jill's body. They're running it through the database. They're running multiple prints through COTIS. The bear hair you found is impregnated with wood smoke and contained some form of human body fluids. They're running DNA tests on that now."

Tony shrugged. "Good stuff most of the time, but it doesn't help me a bit out here."

***

Tony tracked until he could no longer see. They set up camp in the shelter of a fallen pine tree, next to the creek. Every valley had a creek at this time of year. After the snow disappeared, so did many of the creeks. Tony put three-way hobbles on both horses and strapped the feed bags on while Garret gathered firewood.

"It's safe to build a fire?"

Tony nodded. "If they had been close to home, they wouldn't have camped. Even if they aren't far, they're traveling northwest. The wind's from the northwest. It'll blow the smell away from them."

"Good. I'll get plenty of wood. Hope I can sleep."

"Those sleeping bags are supposed to be good to twenty below. I'll cut some branches and lace them in with the others to give us a little more shelter. Put the fire ring just far enough out so we don't catch the place on fire."

"Rocks?"

"Yeah." He smiled. "You remember how to build a fire?"

"I think I can handle it."

They worked in silence. The trunk of the tree had broken five feet above the ground. Using his hatchet, Tony cut the branches from the underside and lay them on the north side of the tree, effectively blocking the wind. Two sleeping bags fit nicely, with the fire pit just beyond the overhanging branches.

Tony removed the feed bags to let the horses graze, then broke out the cooking supplies. He used branches to hang his little cooking pot over the fire, then handed Garret utensils and a Meal Ready To Eat. Garret read the label.

"Ah-h, good old MRE's. Beef stew. I've eaten a lot of these. When you need 'em, they sure hit the spot."

"Yeah. I'm looking forward to the hot chocolate."

"Sounds good. How much food did you bring?"

"Enough for five days."

"Five? This isn't supposed to be a rescue mission."

"Then why didn't we call in the troops when we found the trail?"

"Good question. Then we'd have to have enough food for a posse. Better to get a closer fix on where our kidnappers have gone to ground before we bring in the troops."

Tony nodded and finished chewing the candy bar from the MRE. "Great minds think alike. And I brought five days worth of food because I believe in being prepared for things like late spring storms."

"That's why I like you. By the way, you're on the FBI payroll now."

"Oh. Hadn't thought about that. Working for the FBI today, sheriff's department yesterday, and the park service the day before. I wear many hats."

He poured hot water on the beef stew. Garret laughed while he stirred his supper.

"Right now, I'll bet your glad you're wearing that stocking cap. Is it too early to worry about bears?"

"Yeah. In this part of the country."

"Good. At least that won't keep me awake. Now the cold and worrying about homicidal mountain men, those might keep me awake."

"We're not close to their home."

"What makes you say that?"

"Like I said, they camped back there. If they'd been close to home they'd have kept going. But I also think they'll get more cautious when they get close to their hangout. Not want to leave a trail for anyone to follow."

"I'm sleeping with my Glock anyhow."

Tony patted his pistol. "I hear you."

They finished their meals in silence, both wiping up the last of the stew with the bread before pouring water into the hot chocolate. Garret wrapped his hands around the cup and asked another of those questions designed to sharpen Tony's investigation skills.

"Why did they take the girls?"

Tony had already asked himself that question. "The same reason men usually want women."

"Yeah. But there's three of them. Why didn't they take Mrs. Fisher?"

"I've thought about that ever since we discovered there were three. Why kill her? Why not take one for each of them? They raped her." He stared at his cup for a moment. "What did the coroner say? Did all three rape her?"

"Just one set of DNA."

Tony drank. "So the girls were for the other two. Maybe a father and two sons. The sons are getting restless up in the mountains. The father takes them out looking for women. The sons want wives, but their father has been there, done that. He figures Jill will be too hard to control, so he rapes and kills her. I've had this awful picture of the girls watching all that. But I think they were long gone before their parents were murdered."

"Sons took the girls and left their father behind to do the dirty work.

That's a good possibility. If they wanted the girls as wives, they'd probably try to minimize the trauma. Might even tell them that their parents were still alive. Threaten to go back and kill them if the girls got out of line."

Tony poured more water into his cup, swirled it to get the last bit of chocolate, and drank the contents.

"Do you think the girls will believe that?"

"Probably depends on how strong their denial is. You know them. What do you think?"

"I barely know them. They're smart girls. One's a junior. The other's a sophomore. I can't remember which is which. They'll know these guys killed their parents."

"Let's hope we can get them home alive. And let's hope these sleeping bags are as good as you claim. We need our beauty rest."

Tony chuckled. "Especially you."

V

Tony woke to a gloomy, gray morning. A light dusting of snow covered the ground and clouds shrouded the ridges around them. He unzipped the sleeping bag just enough to add wood to the fire, then zipped himself in again while he waited for the blaze to build. Garret stirred.

"How'd you sleep?" Tony asked.

"Not bad under the circumstances. I was warm enough. Your shelter kept the snow off us. Did we get enough to interfere with tracking?"

"No. Good thing too. It's not going to melt today."

He unzipped the sleeping bag to his waist and sat up. He had left his canteen and the cooking pot full of water close enough to the fire to keep them thawed. He hung the kettle over the flames and rummaged in his saddle bags.

"What's for breakfast?"

"How does peanut butter sandwiches and more hot chocolate sound?"

"It's not bacon and eggs, but it'll fill the empty spot."

"I'm saving the bacon and eggs for another time."

"Right."

After eating, they saddled and watered the horses, then broke camp. Tony tracked on foot until he felt sure of his trail.

The wind velocity increased. Throughout the morning, snow squalls lasting a minute or two passed over them once or twice an hour. The mini blizzards could be seen moving down the valley, though Tony rarely noticed until a near whiteout surrounded them. These forced him to dismount in order to see the tracks.

At 11:30, they found another campsite. This one showed signs of previous habitation. A lean-to about twenty feet long had been built against a rock outcrop. Evergreen branches covered the roof, camouflaging it from the air. A fire pit even had a grate, an old oven rack. An ammunition box inside the lean-to held kindling, matches, and jerky.

"I'd bet we're about a day's hike from their home," Tony said. "We don't want to disturb anything here."

"But they'll know we've been here anyhow."

"Yeah. If they come this way in the near future. We might go unnoticed, but the horses are hard to miss. Let's just pray that they don't come this way before we find them."

They moved on. Within fifteen minutes, the snow started again. This time, it did not stop. Tony had been following a well used trail along the creek because, once again, their quarry had left no tracks in the morning. Now he called a halt.

"We're so close. We could probably find them before nightfall."

"The two of us don't want to find them. We'd probably surprise them. But these guys have more experience in this country than you do. I'd hate to surprise two of them and have the other one running loose. Or two of them. Or find their place while they're out gathering firewood."

Tony nodded and opened his map under the shelter of a spruce tree. He marked the spot where they had found the camp, then studied it for a moment. He closed the map and pointed uphill to their right.

"We go that way."

Garret looked up, seeing only snow and clouds. "If you say so."

"There should be a saddle in the ridge, making it easier to cross into the valley where we'll find that cabin."

"Let's go. This snow isn't getting any lighter."

They mounted and urged the horses along as fast as they could safely move. As they climbed, they found that Tony's navigation was only about a quarter mile off. They rode across the slope to the saddle, with the northwest wind pushing them along. Once over the crest, the ridge provided some shelter.

Garret called a stop to check in, knowing he might not have a signal at a lower elevation. He gave the approximate location where they had left the trail and their destination. The agent he spoke to would have the same map Tony carried. Garret also asked them to check on any reports of encounters with "mountain men" in a fifty square mile area.

He disconnected. "They say the storm's still supposed to hit about nightfall. I'd call what we're in a storm."

"This is nothing." Tony nudged Chance down the slope.

One of the ever-present creeks spilled off the saddle into the valley. The map had failed to show the dense vegetation there. They could not follow the creek, instead skirting thick growths of lodgepole pine and aspen. The horses scrambled up and down the banks of large washes and jumped smaller ones.

And still, the snow fell, heavier as the day progressed. Several inches accumulated. Tony prayed. They could survive if they did not find the cabin intact. But it would be a struggle. And it would be far from a sure thing. A cabin would make surviving the storm much easier.

***

Dusk came early under the low clouds and snow. In places, the horses waded through knee deep drifts. But the valley widened and the trees thinned, making it possible for Tony to follow the creek. He knew that they would have to stop and make a shelter soon if they did not find the cabin. Before long, he would not have enough light to travel. He began looking for potential shelters.

He nearly missed it.

The cabin sat farther from the creek than he had expected and young pine trees had grown up in what must have once been a clearing. It had not been used in years, maybe decades. Shutters which had once covered the windows, hung on loose hinges, but the windows and door remained intact.

Tony dismounted and tied Chance in the shelter of the cabin before he and Garret pushed the door open. He turned on his flashlight, illuminating twenty square feet of cabin with a three foot pile of snow in the southeast corner. A rectangular hole in the roof provided the inlet.

"We can use some of this broken furniture for firewood. But we'll need more. See what you can find under the snow. But don't get lost. I'll cut some of these young trees and make a patch for the roof. Check your watch. I want both of us in the cabin in a half-hour."

"Right."

Tony saw little of Garret during that half hour. He used his hatchet to cut the two to three inch trunks, finding plenty near the southeast corner. He heaved these onto the roof, a tricky procedure given the prevailing wind. When he had a dozen up, he climbed the log ends at the corner of the cabin. Holding on with one hand, he jammed the cut trunks into the snow piled on the slope above the hole, laying the trees across the opening, with the tops draped over the eaves.

He wished that he had left a light on inside so he could see how good a job he had done. As if on cue, a flashlight beam appeared inside the cabin. Only a little light showed through the branches. Tony climbed down and checked his watch. A half-hour had passed. He circled the building, finding quite a pile of dead fall beside the door.

"You collected enough for the night. We can gather more tomorrow when we can see better. Hopefully."

"You did a nice patching job. Hardly any snow's coming through."

"I want to put a few more on. They're close enough to the cabin, I can cut them without getting lost."

"I'll build a fire."

"Run one of the boards from that old bunk up the chimney first. Something probably built a nest in there."

"Do you think of everything?"

"Not always."

By the time Tony placed a half dozen more saplings on the roof, Garret had a nice fire burning. They warmed themselves and took a better look at their surroundings. A broken table, chairs, and bunks littered the building. A plank bench to one side of the fireplace must have served as a kitchen counter. Fruit crates nailed above it had served as cupboards. Someone had taken everything salvageable out of it long ago.

"We'll chop all this lumber so it'll fit into the fireplace and stack it over here before we bring the horses in."

"The horses? Couldn't they survive outside?"

"Yeah. But do you have any idea how much body heat two horses give off?"

Garret grinned. "Well, by all means, let's make room for the horses. How do you plan to keep them from stepping on us?"

"I haven't quite figured that out yet."

***

Chance followed Tony inside without hesitation, but the black gelding took a little more coaxing. Tony spent ten minutes tapping his hind quarters with a stick, eventually building up to a pretty good smack before the horse joined Chance. Then he danced around a while in the small space before Chance warned him to behave with pinned-back ears.

After a thorough search, Tony finally found a place to tie both animals, insuring that they would stay on their side of the cabin. He unsaddled and handed the equipment to Garret, then strapped on the feed bags.

"Sorry, boys. This is all you get till morning."

"I didn't ask how much food you brought for them."

"Grain for two more days. But they need more feed than that.

Tomorrow we have to get them out where they can dig through the snow for grass."

"They can't do that in hobbles."

"No. I'll have to picket one with the lariat and leave the other loose. With any luck, we'll still have both of them at the end of the day."

"If horses behave like horses."

"Right. Now we can eat."

"It's about time. What's on the menu tonight?"

"How does chili sound?"

"Anything. Will we need to hunt for food?"

"I have some wire to make a snare. And I have fish hooks and line. This creek should be big enough to have some fish in it. We'll do that tomorrow."

"How long you think we'll be here?"

Tony shrugged. "Depends on how long the storm lasts. How much snow we get. How fast it warms up afterward. My guess is, I should have brought more food."

"Oh. I guess we'd better hunt and fish then. We've seen a lot of deer. You don't want to shoot one?"

"I don't want to take the chance that the bad guys will hear it, however remote. I'd like them to get comfortable and not worry that they were followed."

"When we make contact with civilization again, I'll use my connections to get the military to send an Unmanned Aerial Vehicle over this area, with infrared cameras. Unless they're in a cave somewhere, that will find them."

"You can do that?"

"Does that surprise you?"

"I suppose it shouldn't. Why didn't we do that first?"

"I had to give them some idea where to look. And now I know how many they need to look for."

"Okay. You started me thinking I was trapped here for no reason."

"You've served your purpose."

VI

Tony, accustomed to camping with horses, slept well that night. The animals' body heat combined with the fire, kept the cabin comfortable, much warmer than the previous night. He could also relax, with no concern that the killers would surprise them. The wind howling around the cabin did not disturb him. He only woke when he heard Garret moving about the next morning.

He stretched. "Why are you up so early? No place to go."

"Our noisy roommates kept me awake half the night."

"You'll get used to it. Are the jeans dry?"

"Yeah. But pretty cold. I'm waiting till the fire builds a little before I put mine on."

"Good plan."

"So what do we do this morning? I guess traveling is out."

Tony glanced at the frosted window. "As soon as it gets light, we'll take the horses out. I've rethought my plan. I'll picket Joker, but I won't exactly leave Chance loose. I'll fasten the three way hobble to his hind leg, then tie the lead rope to it. He'll be able to eat. But if he tries to run, he'll jerk his head. I'll just feel better."

"I like the idea of having horses when we're ready to leave."

"I'll find a place to set up a snare, then try to catch a fish while you gather more firewood. Then I think we can come in till it's time to bring the horses back. I can study the map. Figure out where we go from here."

"Okay. More peanut butter sandwiches for breakfast?"

"How about that bacon and eggs?"

"You were serious?"

"Well, it's powdered eggs, but the bacon's real. Kelly and I fry up a bunch of it, then freeze it in small packages. It's not so heavy and keeps a little better. I brought quite a bit along and I didn't count that when I said I had five day's rations. So we're good for a couple more days, even if we don't catch anything."

"Break out the bacon and eggs. Glad I brought you along."

***

After they found a location where the horses could paw for grass, Tony searched for a place for his snare. To his surprise, he spotted rabbit tracks under some low hanging evergreen branches. With snow still falling and the wind whipping it, the tracks had to be very recent. But he still set his snare with little hope of success.

He picked up a sturdy stick, then walked along the creek until he located a deep pool. He tied his fishing line to the stick and threw the lure in. Sitting would have meant soaking more of his body. The wet snow had already worked it's way through to his skin to well above his knees. He paced back and forth to stay warm.

Garret walked by dragging a ten foot long branch. He grinned. "I'm freezing my butt off and I'm moving. Don't stay out here too long."

"I'll give it another half hour. I'll check my snare and the horses before I come in."

Garret checked his watch. "Okay. I'll gather wood that long. See you in forty five minutes."

Tony kept pacing. He saw trout in the pool, but they did not seem hungry this morning. He gave up a little short of the half hour. He removed the line from the stick, and stuffed it into the pocket of his parka. Then he used the stick to assist him in wading through the snow.

He reached the horses first. Both Chance and Joker dug through the snow, tearing out big mouthfuls of the long, dry grass. He felt relieved. They would find enough to keep them satisfied. No doubt they would lose weight on this trip, but they would not starve to death. He only hoped that no cougars hunted this area. Mountain lions liked nothing better than horse meat.

He slogged on to his snare, then searched for it for the next ten minutes. Everything looked the same in the snow and blowing snow. To his unending surprise, he found a snow shoe hare caught in it. He said a prayer of thanks and reset the snare before heading back to the creek. Following it would provide the easiest route to the cabin.

By the time he stumbled in the door, he felt exhausted.

"Come over here by the fire," Garret said. "I was getting worried about you. What you got there?"

Tony held up the rabbit and Garret took it.

"Sorry. No fish."

"Rabbit's great. I'll clean it."

"Tomorrow, I'll use some of the guts on my fish hook."

Tony warmed his hands for a few minutes before stripping off his wet clothes and hanging them by the fire. He slipped into his sleeping bag and huddled there as the cold began seeping out of him. Garret returned with the cleaned, skinned rabbit and a straight, hardwood stick. He pushed the rabbit into the snow in the corner of the cabin and began sharpening the stick.

"It's still warm. It'll be better if we let it cool off. You're shivering. Want some hot chocolate?"

"Just give me a cup of warm water. It'll do the trick."

Garret poured for him, then resumed whittling. "You were right about the horses. It's a lot colder in here without them. I don't even mind the eau du horse manure."

Tony drank. "We'll bring them back in before dark and put them out in the morning."

"I think you should just stay here and let me bring them in."

"I'll be fine by then."

"And you'll get chilled again. I don't need you sick. Just rest till tomorrow."

"It's really a two-man job. You need to stop by the creek and see if they want a drink."

"I can handle it. There. Looks sharp enough to skewer a rabbit. How you doing?"

"Better. Why don't you bring that map over."

They sat with their backs to the fire, the map held between them. Tony pointed to a line of dashes crossing the valley east of their location.

"Is that supposed to be a road?" Garret asked.

"Unimproved. I'd say an old logging road. Maybe hasn't been used for as long as this cabin."

"There could be nothing left of it."

"Could be. But it may make our trip out of here a little easier. It's about five miles from here." He studied the map a little longer. "Then six or seven miles to an improved road. And this," he tapped the map. "Should be a ranch. About two more miles."

"So we're only about fourteen miles from civilization."

"More or less. You should be able to make contact before we get there."

"Whenever that is. Wish I'd asked how long this storm was supposed to last."

"Spring storms usually move fast. I'm guessing it'll blow over before the end of the day. I hope so anyhow."

***

"So the guy says, 'You've burned my waffles for the last time!'"

Even Garret had to laugh at his own joke. Tony laughed until he had to wipe tears away.

"Thanks. After the past few days, I needed a laugh."

Garret took another bite of rabbit and chewed it before speaking again.

"I thought so. In this job, you need some kind of release. I collect jokes. It's healthier than going home and beating my wife."

Tony looked up from tending the fire. "Does that really happen?"

"Yeah. Unfortunately. What's bothering you, Tony?"

"You mean, besides having seen friends murdered and thinking about what those animals are doing to their daughters?"

"Yeah. You're a professional. You can handle that. As a matter of fact, you were always able to handle it. That's what put you on my radar the first time I met you. You'd seen a man half eaten by a bear, but you were so cool. I thought no one who hadn't seen a lot of death should be able to handle that."

Tony shrugged. "You know it's my faith. Death is a part of life. But it's a little different when you know the victims. It was even hard with those agents that Gil killed up in Montana. I barely knew them."

"Yeah. It's tougher when it's someone you know. But that's not what's bothering you. You've dealt with that. I could see that when we talked about why these guys took the girls." He just waited for Tony to answer.

"Do you think maybe I ... get some kind of ... I don't know ... perverse thrill from seeing murder victims?"

Garret laughed. "You? No. You're the last person who'd do that. Why would *you* think that?"

"Well. Um-m. This time, and after I found Martini's body ... I've had ... the wildest sex of my life."

Garret laughed again. "That's your release, Tony. You deal with it in bed. So when you found the guy the bear had eaten, you were like a monk. What did you do that time?"

"The thought crossed my mind. Kelly had just come back into my life. If you had given me any time, I might have been tempted. But between sleep deprivation, interrogation, and spending time in jail, I got over it." He smiled. "You have no idea what a relief it is to hear that I'm not some kind of pervert."

"Only you would worry about that. I'll bet if you think about it, there are other times that didn't involve murder when you reacted the same way."

Tony thought. "Yeah. That's probably why we have Brett. I'd just rescued Kelly from that flood. At least that probably got me started. After the first time, I was just enjoying myself. Then, after Gil shot me. When I got out of the hospital, I did way more in bed than I should have. I slept a long time after that session."

"So you're just a perfectly normal guy who needs to do something life affirming after something terrible happens."

"Thanks for prying that out of me. I was afraid to talk to anybody about it. I think I'd better explain it to Kelly before she starts thinking the same thing I did."

"Probably not a bad idea. You think it's time to bring the horses in."

"Close enough. I'll help you."

"I told you to stay here. I think it's even getting a little lighter out there. I'll be fine."

"Well, let's take a look before we make that decision."

When Garret opened the door, they even saw patches of blue sky above the blowing snow. They both grinned and Garret gave the order.

"It's still nasty out there, but I can see the horses. Stay here."

"Yes, sir."

***

They spent another comfortable, restful night in the cabin. Tony woke just enough to notice that the wind had died, then rolled over and slept until daylight. This time, Garret did not stir before he did.

Tony dropped some well-rotted wood on the embers in the fireplace. It smoldered for a moment before bursting into flame. He added sticks and finally larger pieces before hanging the kettle of water over the flames.

Garret groaned and sat up. "I slept like a rock. But I'm really stiff. I'll be glad to see a mattress again."

"It's not so bad. But I probably do this a little more than you do."

"And you're probably fifteen years younger than I am."

"I suppose that helps too." Chance nickered. "I'll get them out to eat before we do. And this time, you get to stay inside. I'll check my snare while I'm out."

"Okay. I'll have breakfast ready when you get back."

Tony opened the door to brilliant sunshine. "Hey. I just thought of something. Since this valley runs east and west, the snow will melt faster. It should settle a lot today. We'll try to get moving before sunrise tomorrow. If the Lord smiles on us, we should be able to make it to that ranch in one day."

"Sounds good to me."

VII

They both woke well before sunrise the next morning. Tony saddled the horses and put them out to graze before returning to the cabin for breakfast. They doused the fire and closed the cabin door, leaving it in better shape than they had found it. The eastern sky turned pink as they followed the creek down the valley.

Dense vegetation sometimes impeded the horses, but hidden washes were more often a problem. The snow had drifted evenly over the smaller washes, making them appear level. The third time Chance foundered in belly deep snow, Tony began noticing the telltale signs that a gully lay beneath the snow. They could not avoid them, but he tried to pick an easier way for the horses to cross.

Three miles from the cabin, the forest suddenly changed from old growth timber of mixed hard and soft woods to solid pine trees between twenty and thirty feet tall and smaller, younger hardwood trees. They looked at each other and smiled.

"Never thought an old logged area would be such a welcome sight," Garret said.

In this dense, young growth the snow lay thicker, but the valley had widened. Tony rode southeast, away from the creek, encountering fewer washes. The horses worked harder in the heavy snow. He stopped often to rest them.

They did not see the road until they stood on it. Smaller trees had crept in from its shoulders, making it doubtful that a pickup could use the track. But two horses could walk abreast.

Garret laughed. "I think God's smiling down on us."

Tony coughed. "It's already noon. We have a long way to go."

"Looks like the snow has settled more here. Should be easier for the horses."

"They need a break. If we find some real easy going, we'll get off and walk."

"Let's rest on that ridge ahead. I'll call in."

The horses either sensed that they were headed home, or appreciated the easier going. Their pace increased. Near the crest of the ridge, bare ground appeared. The wind had swept most of the snow away and the rest had melted. They dismounted and let the horses graze. While Tony studied the land through binoculars, Garret called in.

"Yeah. We're still alive. Let our wives know. Get a fix on my position ... Okay, I want you to send up a UAV. You know who to call. Search northwest of my previous position. Look for any signs of current habitation ... No more than ten to twenty miles ... Also, have you contacted the LEOs in a fifty mile radius? ... Good. I want them to question every rancher in that area about any contact with mountain men or survivalists. They either have to trade for or steal supplies somewhere ... Our map shows what looks like a ranch southeast of us, maybe seven or eight miles. Maybe you could give them a heads up to expect us ... It'll be dark before we get there. Talk to you from there."

Garret disconnected and Tony offered him bacon.

"I think I can see the improved road way off in the distance."

"I'm feeling better already. Want to walk the horses a while?"

"Yeah. Let's go."

They walked a half mile downhill before mounting again. As the afternoon progressed, Tony began coughing more often. Garret watched him, but saw no point in mentioning his concern. They could expect no improvement in Tony's condition until they reached a warm, dry place. That could only be accomplished by pushing on.

Just before sunset, the logging road ended at what seemed to them a thing of beauty. A graded road, with trees cleared well away from the shoulders. The snow had not been plowed, but a snowmobile had come to this point from the south, then returned, providing a packed trail for the horses to follow.

"You think they did this because they knew we were coming?" Garret asked.

"Yeah." Even a one word answer started Tony coughing.

"You're looking kind of gray."

"That good?"

For the next mile, only his coughing broke the rhythmic sound of the horses' hooves crunching snow. Garret dismounted to open a barbed wire gate when a cattle guard blocked the road.

Tony grinned. "You sure you know how to operate one of those things?"

"I thought a barbed wire fence was the Texas state tree till I started school." Tony's laugh deteriorated to coughing. Garret mounted and pointed ahead to a glow in the darkness. "That must be the ranch."

"Thank God."

Within a few yards, both horses raised their heads and whinnied. At least two answers came from the ranch. The geldings responded by increasing their pace, moving as if on springs. Tony and Garret had to hold them back, a tough job for two tired men. The calls back and forth between the horses continued until they turned into the sprawling ranch yard.

The residents had evidently left every light on for them. Four yard lights, as well as outside lights on the house and garage, illuminated their path. A man descended the front steps of the ranch house.

"Welcome, boys. We got a call to expect ya. Climb down. Supper's waiting."

"Thank you, Mr. ..." Garret said.

"Tom Gibson."

"Wyatt Garret. And this is Tony Wagner."

"I don't mean to be rude. But the guy who called said he was with the FBI. Said you two were FBI agents, after those killers. I'm a little skittish with all hell breaking loose around here. Can I see some ID before I send you in the house with my wife?"

"Perfectly reasonable."

Garret dismounted and handed Gibson his ID. After scrutinizing the picture, he returned it.

"I'll take care of your horses. You go on in. I'll bring your saddle bags back to the house."

Mrs. Gibson waited for them on the porch. Tony coughed as he plodded up the steps.

"You going to make it?" Garret asked.

"I've made it this far. I'm not going to quit now."

"Oh, you poor thing," Mrs. Gibson said. "You sound terrible. Come in and we'll get some hot food into you. Hang your coats here in the entryway. Put your boots on the boot driers and have a seat by the table."

"Thank you, ma'am," Garret said. "I'm afraid we smell pretty rank."

"Oh, I've smelled worse. You can get showers after supper."

"That sounds almost as good as your cooking smells."

"There's plenty of chicken and dumplings. We expected the kids home this weekend, but this storm changed that. They hate having to stay in town on the weekends."

"Your kids work in town?"

She laughed. "No. They stay in town during the week to go to school."

"How far are you from town?"

"Thirty-three miles."

"You don't live in the middle of nowhere, but you can see it from here."

She chuckled. "That's a good description."

Her husband rejoined them and poured coffee all around before taking a seat.

"You boys have had quite an adventure. Any sign of those girls?"

"We were getting close when this storm hit. We'll go out again when the snow melts."

"You really think those girls are still alive?"

"We're pretty sure of it. If they intended to kill the girls, they would have done it when they killed the parents."

"Good point."

"Have you had any contact with these guys over the years? Even anything suspicious?"

Gibson sipped his coffee. "No. Don't think so."

"Tom," Mrs. Gibson said. "What about that calf? The one somebody butchered."

"Yeah. That could of been them. About four, five years ago. The boys and I were checking cattle up along that old logging road you came in on. Must have been August. It was hot. We heard a shot and went to check it out. Met up with some of our cows, all spooked and a calf missing. Now we lose a few calves to cats every year. But we backtracked their trail and found where somebody had butchered out the calf and carried away the carcass."

"Did you follow them?"

"Hell, no. I had my boys to think about. But it did start me wondering how many of those losses we blamed on cats might have been the work of two-legged hunters."

Tony coughed and Mrs. Gibson patted him on the shoulder. "I'll put the vaporizer in your room and give you some hot lemonade and whisky before you go to bed."

Garret grinned. "Does the reverend drink?"

Tony nodded. "My mom used to give me that for a cold when I was a kid."

The Gibsons looked at each other. He spoke.

"The reverend? Not *The* reverend? Well, that's a dumb question. Of course, you have to be *The* reverend. Who else would you be? When they told me to expect a couple of FBI agents, I thought we'd be getting a couple of city boys."

Tony shook his head. "You didn't get even one city boy. He's from Texas. I didn't think anybody outside of Benson County had heard of me."

"I think everybody in this part of Colorado knows about you. I feel better already, knowing you're on this case."

"Thanks." Tony coughed. "Ma'am, you're an awfully good cook. And it was a really nice change from MREs and rabbit. And I don't want to be rude. But now I think I'll take that shower."

"Oh, let me get you some clothes. I couldn't set them out ahead of time because I didn't know how big you'd be. You put your clothes in the basket in the bathroom and I'll wash them tonight. Just clean out your pockets. I won't even do that for Tom. Bathroom's second door on your right. There's disposable razors on the back of the sink."

When she left the kitchen, Tony rubbed his beard and placed his Beretta on the table. She met him at the bathroom door with a stack of clothes, then rejoined her husband and Garret. She topped off their coffee cups.

"Is he always so quiet?"

"No. He's feeling pretty tough. I've been worried about him. Glad he can sleep in a warm bed tonight. Just what have you heard about him?"

"His name was all over the papers when he solved that serial killer case,"

Tom replied. "But I couldn't remember it. That 'reverend' nickname kind of sticks in your mind though. Since then we've heard about other cases he's helped solve. People say he could be a detective in any big city he wanted to. But he likes small town life. He likes spending most of his time being a park ranger, so he doesn't get as many cases as the detectives in Denver. They say we're lucky to have him out here. Maybe his reputation keeps some criminals from coming this way."

Garret shrugged. "It can't hurt. I'd say they're right about one thing. He could be a detective anywhere. Or an FBI agent. I tried to talk him into that, back before I knew better."

"The fella on the phone," Tom said. "Told us you were both FBI agents."

"Just trying to keep it simple. Tony is an FBI consultant. I've dragged him all over the country when I needed someone for rock climbing or tracking. But he's more than a hell of a tracker. I get an extra investigator when I bring him along. And more important, I get an investigator who isn't a city boy."

"That must have come in pretty handy this time."

"Every time. One case turned into a murder investigation just because he looked at pictures. The coroner ruled it an accident. A guy had been trampled by a herd of horses. All the evidence seemed to point to it. His body was surrounded by hoof prints. The agents were about to close the case. Just to cover their butts, they showed the crime scene and autopsy pictures to Tony. Right away he started asking questions about the herd. When he got the answers, he said, 'It's murder.' Of course, they needed more than that."

"What'd he see?"

"Shoe prints. The shoes even had some kind of toe and heel caulks for traction. The horses in that area got caught about once a year for vaccinations and what have you. They were barefoot. The prosecutor called him as an expert witness on that case."

"It's quite an honor to have both of you as our guests."

"Well, we appreciate your hospitality. Not to sound ungrateful. But when can we get out of here?"

Tom chuckled. "Plow's supposed to come out tomorrow. Your people will probably be waiting at the county shop to follow it. We're getting the royal treatment with you here. These spring storms, the county usually just makes us wait till the snow melts."

They talked about the Gibson's three children until Tony returned from his shower, clean shaven and dressed in sweat pants and a t-shirt.

Mrs. Gibson smiled. "Oh, now I recognize you from your pictures in the paper. The beard makes a good disguise."

Tony chuckled. Garret handed him his phone.

"Got a pretty good signal. Call your wife."

"Did you call yours?"

"No. She's been married to an FBI agent for a long time. She doesn't expect to hear from me when I'm gone."

"M-m. If you folks will excuse me." He retreated to another room and checked the signal before calling home. "I love you, Kelly."

"Tony! You sound funny."

"I have a cold."

"Oh. I love you. Ryan told me you'd make it to a ranch tonight. We've been worried about you."

"No need to worry. We had plenty of warning before the storm hit. The map showed us where to find shelter. We just got kind of sick of our own cooking."

"When will you be home?"

"How's tomorrow sound?"

"It sounds great. Oh, Brett wants to talk to you."

Twelve-year-old Brett came on the line. "You okay, Dad?"

"Yeah. Just got a little cold."

"Did you catch those guys?"

"Not yet. The storm got in our way."

"You going after them again?"

"Somebody is. But not for a few days."

"Christina wants to say hi."

Five year old Christina took the phone from her brother. "Hi, Daddy."

"Hi, sweety. Have you been helping Mommy?"

"Yeah."

"How's you're little brother?"

"Fine."

"I'll be home tomorrow."

"See you."

Abruptly, Kelly came back on the line. "I wish she talked so little all the time. I miss you."

"I miss you too. I have to go. I'm really tired."

"Get some rest. I'll see you tomorrow. I love you."

"Love you too."

VIII

Tony's coughing only disturbed him infrequently and briefly that night. He woke with the sun shining in the bedroom window. After searching for his clothes, he remembered that Mrs. Gibson had washed them the night before. He yawned and stopped in the bathroom before descending the stairs.

Garret sat at the kitchen table, fully dressed. Tony took the coffee that Mrs. Gibson offered him.

"Thanks. Sorry I slept so late."

"Did you have a reason to get up early?"

"No, ma'am. I guess I didn't."

"Well, then don't apologize. How do you feel this morning?"

"Like I have a cold. But I feel a lot better than I did last night. Thanks for the great hospitality. And thank your son for the use of his room."

"You're very welcome. How about some pancakes and sausage?"

"Sounds good. I'd better get dressed."

"Yeah," Garret said. "You don't want me to tell our ride that he has to wait because you're still in your jammies."

Tony made a face before he left the room.

They had barely finished breakfast when a vehicle back up alarm sounded. Tom hurried to the window.

"There's the plow. He turns around here because no one else lives down this road. And that must be your ride pulling in the yard. You boys just stay put. I'll get your horses loaded." He held up a hand when they tried to protest. "No arguments. Get your boots and coats on."

They thanked Mrs. Gibson and reached the barn just as Tom and a man Tony did not recognize loaded the last of their equipment. Garret offered to pay for their room and board.

Tom declined with a laugh. "Gave us an exciting tale to tell."

"Well, we thank you and the Bureau thanks you. You'll probably see us again in a few days."

Tony climbed into the back seat of the Yukon and Garret introduced him to Agent Mc Cormick. Tony acknowledged him, then tried to listen to their conversation about pictures the UAV had taken. But his mind wandered to the sixty mile drive ahead of them. He dozed off within minutes.

Garret took him to the urgent care/trauma center at Spruce Lake, insisting that he see a doctor. Tony declined a prescription for precautionary antibiotics, instead promising to report to the clinic on Tuesday for further evaluation. The doctor prescribed rest until then.

By the time they reached park service housing, Tony again felt exhausted. Kelly ran to him and they hugged on the front sidewalk. Brett and Christina followed.

"Hey. Who's in the house with Justin?"

"He's napping. You look like you're not far behind him."

"M-m."

"He has doctor's orders to rest," Garret said.

"I'll make sure he does."

Tony turned toward Garret. "Wait a minute. What's next?"

"You don't need to worry about that now. I'll come by tomorrow afternoon to brief you."

"Okay." He wrapped his arm around Kelly's shoulders and walked into the house, stopping in the kitchen. She guided him to the bedroom.

"We're glad to have you home, but I think you need to go right to bed. I'll turn off the ringer on the phone in here. Just get some sleep."

"Yes, ma'am."

***

Tony slept the rest of the afternoon and all night. Kelly left for work before he woke the next morning. He walked around the house in a fog until after his first cup of coffee. He ate, showered, and called Kelly at Park Headquarters, suggesting that she come home for lunch.

"But we'll have dessert first."

Kelly chuckled. "Um-m. I haven't had dessert since Tuesday. You sure you're up to dessert?"

"Oh, yeah. I had a couple of boring days in the mountains to think about it?"

"I'll be there."

Tony set the table, made lunch, and changed from clothes to his bathrobe. When Kelly arrived, grinning, he locked the door behind her. They left her uniform and his robe in the kitchen. They ignored the phone ringing. His coughing only once interrupted their pleasure.

She sighed and snuggled into his arms. "I'd like to take the afternoon off for more of this."

"I don't think I'm up to that."

"Probably not."

"Maybe when this is all over."

"Sounds wonderful." She turned to a more serious subject. "Do you think the girls are still alive?"

"Yeah."

"Why?"

"These guys wanted them alive."

"Who took them?"

"Mountain men? Survivalists? Somebody who lives in the wilderness. Somebody who wants female companionship."

"They'll force themselves on Christi and Terri."

He stroked her hair. "Yeah." He kissed her forehead. "We were so close. If that storm hadn't come up, we would have caught up with them. I've been asking myself why God didn't let us catch them."

She squeezed his chest. "I heard there were three of them."

"We found three sets of tracks."

"Maybe you two couldn't handle all three of them. God wanted you to go back for reenforcements."

He rolled over and gave her a very long kiss. "You're right. I should have thought of that. I'd better get your lunch on the table."

"Wear that outfit when you serve lunch." He laughed, but when she joined him in the kitchen, she found him naked. "You'd better put your robe on or I'll be late for work. Oh, we'll be moving about the first of June."

He grabbed the robe. "Roger got the job at Glacier?"

"Yes. So we get the four-bedroom house."

"We need it."

Kelly dressed and ate at the same time. As she tucked in her shirt, the doorbell rang. They both laughed at the close call.

Tony opened the door for Garret. "You're early."

"It's afternoon." He looked from one grinning face to the other, glanced at Tony's robe, then fixed his gaze on Kelly. "Nooner?"

She blushed. "None of your business."

"He had orders to rest. You're jeopardizing the health of one of my operatives. Of course it's my business."

She punched his arm as she passed him. "Then look at the smile on his face. I'm contributing to the morale of your operative."

"Ouch! That's assaulting a federal officer."

"So arrest me." She called back over her shoulder. "Love you, Tony!"

"Love you."

Garret grinned. "Feeling better?"

"As a matter of fact, yeah. What you got there?" Tony nodded to the accordion file under Garret's arm.

"Everything we need to plan this operation. You want to make room to work?"

After Tony cleared the table, Garret spread a map, then handed him an infrared picture. It showed a structure with four hot spots inside.

"People?"

"Yeah."

"But just four."

"The other one may have been off somewhere. But it's them. The UAV didn't find anyone else out there. It's only about a mile from their last campsite, as the crow flies. But they would've had to fly to take that route. Probably about a five mile hike over some pretty rugged going."

"Good reason to have a camp where we found it. They wouldn't want to cross that rugged trail if it was getting close to dark."

"That's what I thought. I've marked the locations on this map."

Tony studied the contours for several minutes. "They picked this location for a reason. We can't take horses in there. Without the UAV, we'd have never found it from the air. If they hadn't kidnaped the girls, they could have stayed hidden for years."

"Sex makes men do stupid things."

"So how do we get them out?"

"I have a team assembled. Ten of us, including you and me. They're collecting horses and equipment. We haul in to the head of the logging road, then ride to the cabin. That becomes our base of operations. We use the UAV again to confirm that they aren't on the move, then make our way to the point where we'll have to leave the horses. Hopefully, we can use the UAV again as a lookout."

"What does the military think about the FBI tying up their multi-million dollar drone?"

"There should probably be a 'b' in front of that. Those things might run into the billions as far as I know. These are called training exercises. Those guys at the controls need to stay sharp. And they need to train in new guys all the time."

"I see. When do we leave?"

"I've talked to meteorologists and locals. As warm as it is, we should be able to move by Thursday. You going to be up to it?"

"Probably."

"If you're not, we'll wait. You're critical to this operation. If they slip away, we'll need you to track them."

"I'll see the doctor again tomorrow. Ask me on Wednesday."

"Done. I won't even bother you tomorrow."

"Where you getting the horses?"

"Neil White and Tom Gibson."

"I want Chance."

"Thought you would."

"What's your plan once we're on foot?"

Garret tapped the map. "You can see that this is a bottle neck."

"Yeah. Perfect place for an ambush."

"That's where the UAV comes in. After we get the all clear, you and I go through. Once we've established defensive positions, we signal the other six to follow. Two will stay with the horses. We surround the cabin and adapt as needed. If we can neutralize one or more of the kidnapers away from the cabin, that would be ideal. If not, we have tear gas and stun grenades."

"I'm sure you have improved communication all worked out."

"State of the art."

"How long do you see this operation taking?"

"Three days. If we catch them at their cabin."

"Feed for the horses?"

"We're taking a pack horse to carry that in. We're going state of the art there too. White's in charge of that department. He's sending along some kind of super ration so they don't have to depend so much on grass."

"Sounds like you have your bases covered. I figured you would. Anything new from forensics?"

"The DNA from the body fluid on the bear hair is a familial match to the guy who raped Jill Fisher. Father and son."

"The father raped her?"

"Yeah. Looks like you called it right. Any other questions?"

"Have you talked to Don?"

"Yeah. Grouchy as ever. He made it real clear that the bureau should be paying for your sick time. He doesn't want you using your sick leave because the bureau is responsible for your illness, not the park service."

Tony grinned. "Sounds like Don."

"I assured him that this wasn't costing the park service a dime. Of course, then he went into a ten minute lecture on how valuable you are and what a hardship it puts on everyone when you're running around helping the FBI. I think he managed a few insults about how we couldn't do anything without you. I'm not sure. I tuned him out after about the first minute or two."

"This is our dead time of year. Cross country skiing is done and the summer tourist season hasn't started. We sit around playing cards half the time."

"Our tax dollars at work."

IX

Tony knew that Kelly did not want him going after the kidnappers again. *But she'd never say it out loud.* She understood that he needed to do this kind of work.

He neither craved danger, nor sought it out. But only a handful of people could track better than he could. It seemed unthinkable not to use that ability in a situation like this.

He had explained this to her only once, but she already understood. She had first seen his willingness to help people, even at the risk of his own life, the day he had braved a flood to rescue her. They had met chest deep in muddy water and she had fallen in love with him.

Kelly thought of all this as he held her after they made love. "I'll miss you."

"M-m. With any luck, I'll be home in three days."

"Be careful."

"I will. I'll wear Kevlar."

"That always makes me feel better. Most of your work with the FBI isn't this dangerous."

"Yeah. But sometimes it's part of the job. The Lord is always with me. I probably have a better chance of being struck by lightning working in the park, than getting shot doing these FBI jobs."

"Now that you mention it, you were working in the park when you were shot."

"And I was wearing Kevlar then. I won't be alone this time. I'll have an army with me."

"Okay. Okay. But when this is all done, we *are* taking that day off. We'll send Brett to school, Christina and Justin to Lois. We'll lock the door and won't answer the phone all day."

"I have a better idea. How about we go to Denver for a weekend? A hotel with room service. We spend the whole time in the room."

"Oh-h, I like the way your mind works."

He gave her a long, soft kiss, then sighed. "I have to get ready or Garret will be pounding on the door."

"I know. I'll turn the coffee on."

***

In spots, the clay that formed the logging road had turned to treacherous slime. But thankfully, enough vegetation had grown over most of the surface to allow horses to avoid those places. Tony led the way, leaving the road before they reached the point where he and Garret had stumbled onto it.

He felt much better prepared for this excursion. And the feeling had nothing to do with the squad of men and equipment behind him. Garret had given him access to all the UAV's pictures, which, fortunately, had included this area. By comparing those to the topographic map, he had been able to choose a route around the densest vegetation.

Their column reached the cabin by early afternoon. Setting up camp included establishing satellite communication. While some of the men cared for the horses and gathered firewood, Tony and Garret watched a live feed from the UAV on a notebook computer. The drone zeroed in on the kidnapers camp, then switched to an infrared camera.

Garret counted out loud. "One. Two. Three. Four. Five. All present and accounted for. Our luck is holding. Tony, you want to see anything specific?"

"The bottleneck. And our route between here and there. I want to know how that snow melt has changed things."

Garret nodded to the technician operating the computer and he relayed the request to the military. Within minutes, the UAV changed course, and a little later they saw their location on the screen.

"Now you know they're serious when they say 'big brother is watching.'"

Tony scanned the sky. "I can't even see it up there. If we'd had to use a helicopter or a small plane, those guys would be long gone."

"Ain't technology wonderful?"

"Usually. I'll study those pictures so we don't have any surprises."

"What time you want to get moving in the morning?"

"Before sunrise. As soon as it starts to get light."

"Okay. I'll spread the word."

***

Tony led them to the bottleneck after having skirted gullies and low places where water had collected. Once again they waited for a report from the drone. This time, only three heat sources registered in the dwelling. Two more were located on the other end of the boulder-strewn bottleneck.

Garret signaled a retreat. Two agents led the horses away, while the other eight took cover, their guns ready. The UAV circled. They waited while the technician watched his computer screen. Finally, he relaxed and reported.

"They've killed something. A deer or an elk. And I guess they're gutting it right where we want to go."

"Any way we can surprise them?" Garret asked.

The technician spent some time studying the screen.

"Not advisable. About a hundred yards of open ground between them and cover."

"Okay. Tony and I will go through and watch until they leave. Then we'll call you in. Just sit tight until you get my signal. After you, Tony."

Long ago an earthquake had torn a fissure through the granite ridge. In the process, huge chunks of rock had crashed to the bottom. Through hundreds of years of erosion, dirt and organic matter had filled in some of the spaces between. But they still had to avoid holes large enough for a horse to fall into.

Tony began to wonder if he should have brought his rock climbing gear. Then he noticed the rope. Just a short piece, maybe twenty feet. It hung from one of the more difficult places. He tested it, then used it to make the climb. At several other particularly arduous places, they found more short ropes, and once a log with steps carved into it.

When they peered over the crest into the canyon beyond, they saw two men bending over a deer carcass. With the sun at their backs, Tony and Garret used binoculars for a better look.

The kidnappers were big men, wearing bear skin coats. Both had dark brown hair and full beards. It became apparent that one had at least twenty years on the other. Probably the father and a son. They picked up their rifles and looped ropes over their shoulders, then began dragging the deer away from the bottleneck.

Tony signaled and Garret followed him down the slope, much easier on this side. One watched the hunters from cover while the other moved. They reached the canyon floor about the time the hunters disappeared into the trees. They waited, listening until they could no longer hear their prey.

Garret reached for his transmitter, but Tony held up his hand, then pointed to his ear. Garret listened. In a moment, he heard it. Off to their left. Stones dislodged by someone in a hurry. Then that same someone breathing hard. They pointed their guns toward the source of the noise.

She broke from cover, wide eyed, dirty, disheveled. The younger Fisher girl. Tony still could not remember if she was Christi or Terri. He signaled Garret by putting his hand over his mouth. Garret nodded. They waited behind a huge boulder, with Garret closer to her. When she passed through the opening, he grabbed her, clamping his hand over her mouth.

She fought. Tony moved into her field of vision, hoping that she would see him as a friend. But she had panicked. Her eyes reminded him of a frightened animal. He tried to speak forcefully while keeping his voice low.

"Christi! Christi, look at me! You know me. I'm Tony. From church."

She stopped struggling. Garret slowly removed his hand from her mouth. "Tony?"

"Yeah. Where's Terri?"

"I'm Terri. They still have Christi. You have to help her."

"We will. But first we have to get you out of here."

"Christi said if I got a chance to escape, I had to go. She said that was our best chance."

"She was right. Let's go." Tony scanned their surroundings. "Can you make it up this slope?"

"Uh-huh."

He turned to Garret. "Help her. I'll watch our backs."

"But you're right behind me. Understand?"

"Just like we came down. Cover to cover."

Tony rested his rifle on the boulder, watching for any sign of movement. Someone would miss Terri very soon and come after her. They only needed enough time to get to the crest of the rock pile. Then her pursuers would be sitting ducks for the FBI team on the other side.

He heard the shot at almost the same time Garret grunted and Terri shrieked. Tony looked up, but could see neither. No reason to be quiet any longer.

"Garret!"

"He just winged me."

"The others heard that. They'll be joining this one. Can you call for backup?"

"Sort of smashed my radio. Can our backup hear if we start shooting?"

"Maybe if you get closer to the crest. Can you keep climbing if I lay down cover fire?"

"Yeah."

"Then go when I start shooting. Ready?"

"Whenever you are. And, Tony, if you get a chance, shoot to kill."

"Right. Go!"

Tony's .270 had a nine round clip. He concentrated his fire at the point where Terri had emerged from the trees. A figure ran, seeking better cover. Tony used the opportunity to dodge away from the fissure. He dropped behind a log before his assailant turned and fired at the spot where he had been. Tony raised his rifle over the log and spotted the shooter. Either cocky or stupid, he had given Tony a clear shot.

He remembered Garret's instruction, then took careful aim. And shot. The shooter fell, grasping his thigh. Almost immediately the first two men dragged him to cover. Tony changed clips and lay down more cover fire. When he used up those shells, he dropped the rifle and pulled out his Beretta.

Other gunfire echoed from above. Garret had reached an elevation where he believed that the rest of the team could hear him. *Good. That should discourage them.*

He thought about the wounded man. His aim had been accurate. He believed that two men aiding a wounded colleague would be less of a threat than two men bent on avenging a dead colleague. *I just have to hold out a little longer.*

Tony felt the cold steel behind his ear. He said a silent prayer. *Thy will be done, Lord.*

"Drop it," a female voice said. He used two fingers to lower the pistol. "Good boy. Now put your hands behind your head." He obeyed. "You got brains. I like that. I got him, Pa!"

Pa? Tony felt stupid. He had missed one.

"Well, bring him here, girl! He shot your brother! Stay in the trees so the other one don't get you. Caleb'll keep him busy while you move."

"You heard Pa! Move it!"

Tony rose and followed the directions of the gun barrel prodding the small of his back. The man he had shot sat against a tree, while the older man pointed his rifle at Tony. He prayed again. *Lord, if it's your will, bring me home to my family. If not, bring me home to you.*

The third man, Caleb, fired a round in Garret's direction.

"Move away from him, girl!" The father said.

"Now wait a minute, Pa. When I got mad cause you didn't bring me a man, you said I could just get my own. Well, guess what? I did. Let me take a look at him before you fill him full of holes. I might want to keep him." She circled, staying out of the line of fire.

Tony thought that she would clean up pretty nice, but she needed that cleaning. Her rat's nest hair made her look crazed. And right now, his life was in her hands.

"Oh, he's awful cute. You ain't shooting him."

"He shot your brother."

"He saved me the trouble. Seth was too busy hightailing it to see that blondie, here, moved. Seth gave him an easy shot. Blondie took real careful aim. Could a killed Seth, but he didn't. That was mighty nice a him."

"What happened to Seth's woman?"

"She got away with that other fella."

"There's probably more a them. He might come in handy. Tie his hands good and tight. Then you wait here. If anyone shows their face, shoot it off. You know where to meet us."

"Right, Pa. But you won't shoot blondie?"

"Not unless he does something real stupid."

After she finished tying Tony's hands, she rubbed his rear end and thigh. She lowered her voice. "Is the rest of you as hard as that?"

I need to string her along to buy time. "Yes."

She giggled and picked up her rifle. "Go on with Pa now and be a good boy so we can have a little fun later. Hey, Pa, here's his sidearm."

He took the Berretta and slung his rifle over his shoulder. "That will be a might handier if he tries anything."

The two men carried Seth between them with Tony walking ahead. Tony studied the thick woods, wondering if he could dodge out of sight before the man fired. Or at least make him miss the first time. They probably would not come after him, having more important things to do.

When they passed the deer carcass, they heard a shot. Tony tensed, ready to sprint into the woods.

"Stop, right there." Tony froze. "You're getting too far ahead."

He glanced over his shoulder at the Berretta pointed at him from about six feet away. The man gestured with it for him to continue. Tony moved on. *He's too close. He couldn't miss at this distance.*

They reached the dwelling, not really a cabin, but a timber structure built partially under a rock overhang. Tony studied it while the father entered. Anyone under the overhang would not have registered as a heat source to the UAV's sensors. *Maybe the daughter didn't come along when they kidnaped the girls.* He began to feel a little less stupid.

Christi Fisher stumbled out of the cabin, her hands bound in front of her, looking as disheveled as her sister. When she saw Tony, her jaw dropped. She finally managed one word.

"Terri?"

"Safe."

The father slapped her. "You know better than to talk to other men. You got your own man. Now help him with Seth."

Christi followed orders, and the father threw a punch at Tony, who ducked aside. But he could not avoid the rifle barrel that landed across his ribs, staggering him.

"You're only alive because my daughter took a shine to you. So you'd better stay on her good side. Don't make nice with my daughter-in-law. Now move."

Tony heard another shot. One person with a rifle could hold back a battalion at that bottleneck. *For how long?* Until dark. Then she would slip away, unnoticed.

They walked past the cabin, across the slab of rock it had been built on. *Seth's leaving a blood trail Garret can follow, even across solid rock.* He heard the sound of falling water.

Well before they reached the waterfall, the rock became treacherous. Water seeped from a wide area of the cliff face above them. *This will wash the blood away. I have to find a chance to leave Garret other signs.*

Everyone moved cautiously. But Christi, handicapped with her burden and tied hands, slipped. Seth swore at her. Before long, Tony almost fell. He followed them as they moved closer to the cliff. He felt gravel under his feet.

He wondered if he should pray that the better footing continued or ask for the slippery surface to slow their escape. *Thy will be done, Lord.*

In a moment, he realized that he was being led under the waterfall. A brief panic swept through him. No one on the FBI team could track over water-washed rock. *I can't even do that. How can I leave a trail? He'll notice if I drop anything.*

Tony glanced at the cliff. He staggered, falling against it, rubbing his body along the moss-covered rocks before he straightened, hoping that he had left some kind of mark.

"You're awful clumsy, boy. Or are you just trying to slow us down? You get to be too much trouble and I don't care how much Sue likes you. A bullet solves my problem. Understand?"

"Yes, sir."

"Now that's a good attitude."

Over time, the waterfall had eroded the cliff base, leaving an overhang. Tony had to duck to avoid hitting his head. Just beyond the waterfall a crevice bisected the rock. Vines covered the entrance to the crevice, making it invisible to anyone looking at the waterfall.

As he slipped through the vines, he grabbed one, then dropped the broken piece before the father passed through the screen.

Christi and the other man, carrying Seth, had to turn sideways to traverse the crevice. Tony's shoulders brushed on both sides. Water seeping from the rock soaked his arms. But the surface he walked on seemed unnaturally smooth. He studied it in the shadows.

These people had taken time preparing their escape route, even filling in the bottom of the crevice with gravel to make egress faster. They had planned for this emergency long before they kidnaped Christi and Terri.

The crevice opened onto a slope covered with a thick stand of pine, making it invisible from this end as well. They climbed to the top of the ridge, then descended a steeper, longer slope on the other side, leaving an easy trail to track on the way down.

Christi gasped for air and staggered under her burden. When she fell again, Tony took a risk. "Let me help with Seth, sir. She's about wore out."

He saw the backhand coming, could have avoided it, but did not. Better the hand than the rifle barrel again. His ribs still hurt. The hand just stung.

"You'd like that, wouldn't you. Give you a chance to slow us down more. Or throw both Seth and Caleb down so you only have me to contend with."

"My hands are tied and you have a gun on me. What good would that do me? She's the one who's slowing you down."

The father considered that, then nodded. Tony moved up to take Christi's place. She gave him a grateful glance. The father shook a finger at her.

"Don't you get any ideas, woman. No matter what he does, you're not getting away like your sister did. We went to too much work to get you."

Tony could have done a better job of carrying Seth with his hands free, but saw no point in asking. So far, no one had bothered to search him, discovering his knife, handcuffs, and ... What else? A map. A picture of Kelly and the kids. His wedding ring.

Would the fact that he was married matter to Sue? *If it does, I'm dead.* He had no way to remove his ring with his hands tied and gloves on. The picture he could explain away. But not the ring. *Unless. I'm a terrible liar. I can tell them that I'm a recent widower.* His life might depend on making them believe that.

He prayed that he did not need to use that tactic.

When they paused for Seth to readjust his grip, Tony heard water, a lot of it. A river. *What river? I need to keep my bearings.* He pictured the map. *The Broken Arrow River.* Near its headwaters. In late summer it would be little more than a creek. But at this time of year, snow melt had turned it into a substantial river.

Just before they reached its bank, Tony saw the raft, camouflaged with branches. They stopped and lowered Seth to the ground. The father gave orders, pointing from Tony to Christi.

"You two sit. Not too cozy. Just close enough so I can keep an eye on the two of you. Caleb, bandage Seth's leg better."

Seth had concerns other than his leg. "What about my woman, Pa?"

"She's gone! And you were supposed to be watching her. Man can't hold on to his woman, don't deserve one. I don't want to hear no more bout it. I go to all the trouble a finding 'em, planning that hunting trip, and bringing 'em back here, and you lose her in less than a month." He made a contemptuous sound. "Woman, you know this guy." He nodded at Tony. "What's his name?"

Christi swallowed. "Tony."

"Who is he?" She looked at Tony. "Don't lie to me. You know what I do to liars."

"He's ... our half-brother."

Tony barely kept the shock off his face. *Why did she say that? How can that help?*

"You're lying, woman. I never saw him round your place."

"No, I'm not! Mom got pregnant when she was a teenager. She gave him up for adoption. Dad didn't really like having him around. It made him think about Tony's father."

Tony recognized Christi's strategy. They would not allow her near a strange man. But they might let her close to her brother. *Smart girl.* He spoke up. "It's the truth."

"I'm not talking to you, boy. What's he do? Why'd they let him come along to find you?"

"He's a Park Ranger. He's had to search for a lot of lost people. And he probably wouldn't take 'no' for an answer. That's the kind of brother he is."

He looked from her to Tony, then crouched and unzipped Tony's coat. He found the knife, then the handcuffs. He held them up for Christi to see.

"Park Ranger, huh?"

"He's a ranger cop. He can arrest people."

"You're lying!"

"I can prove it," Tony said.

"How you going to do that?"

"The back of my holster. It's stamped NPS. Evergreen."

"On your belly." Tony followed orders and the man unclipped the holster from his belt. "Okay, now. Didn't know there was such a thing." He pulled off Tony's gloves and asked Christi another question. "Is he married?"

"Yes."

Tony's heart sank. No chance for a lie now. He prayed that it would not matter.

"We'll have to see what Sue thinks bout that." He dug through Tony's coat pockets, finding the map and the little acrylic framed picture. He chuckled. "Okay. Tell me all about his kids."

Tony held his breath, wondering how much Christi really knew about him.

"He has three. Brett. Christina. And Justin's just a baby."

Tony let his breath out.

"Okay. So he's your brother."

He stood and unfolded the map, occasionally making sounds of approval. Caleb finished bandaging his brother and asked about it. "What's so special bout that map, Pa?"

"Big brother, here, knows the mountains. Got the easiest route marked from that old hunting cabin to our canyon. But how did he know we were here? How bout that, big brother?"

"We tracked you a little past your camp. That lean to with the ammo box. But we lost you in the storm. We came back the easier way after the snow melted."

"Nobody could track us. You're lying."

"You're cocky. You left enough signs."

The man kicked him in the ribs, knocking the wind out of him. "I don't like a smart mouth, boy. You just tell me what kind of signs we left."

Tony had to wait until he caught his breath. "The girls hair caught on trees. Bear hair on a tree trunk, but no other sign that a bear had been there. It was enough to keep me on the right trail till the ground thawed out enough for you to leave tracks."

Tony knew that he had slipped up. Any hope that the man had not noticed, vanished. He poked Tony with his rifle barrel.

"So that's why they brought you along. You're the tracker." He laughed. "So we got their eyes. This day ain't turned out half-bad after all."

X

When Garret and Terri crossed the crest of the boulder field, he began firing ineffectively. But it got the attention of his men. He filled them in, then they all waited in frustration while somebody kept them pinned down. *Where's Tony? He should have had enough ammunition to keep that shooter occupied.*

Someone bandaged the deep crease on his left arm, then Garret had the same man escort a nearly hysterical Terri back to the horses.

Garret mumbled a prayer. "I know I don't do this as much as I should, but take care of Tony. Kelly will kill me if I let anything happen to him. And I don't know if I could live with myself."

All afternoon, the sniper only fired enough shots to keep them from entering the canyon. Garret ordered someone to bring him the radio and called in the UAV. But bad weather at its base prevented take off. Conditions were not expected to improve until after midnight.

Garret swore.

The sun set and dusk began to settle. One of his men reported that they had entered the canyon without being fired upon.

"Of course. They slipped away in the dark. Let's go." When he reached the floor of the canyon, someone spotted Tony's rifle. "He moved. He was over there when we climbed out. He saw what a trap that is." He searched the ground with his flashlight. "No blood. He spent both clips, then used his side arm. Look around. See if he moved again. And look for tracks."

He felt helpless. *Where's Tony? Is he on the trail?* No. Tony knew the odds. He would not take unnecessary risks. He would have waited and covered them when they entered the canyon. *He's either dead or captured.* Neither prospect appealed to him, but he prayed for the latter.

Tony would have stuck close to the bottleneck. So if they had killed him, he would not be far. The thought cheered him slightly. *If he was dead, we would have found his body by now.*

"I got tracks!" One of the men called.

Garret hurried to the sound, then pointed his flashlight at the same spot where the agent directed his beam.

"These are Tony's. And look how something has rubbed out part of the print. Someone wearing moccasins stepped on top of his boot print. Someone with a pretty small foot. They were following him. Probably had a gun on him. Everybody over here. We have to wait till morning or we'll just wipe out the trail." He studied the terrain in the gathering darkness. "Set up a defensive position."

"What about the girl, sir?"

"She can stay where she is for the night. I need volunteers to go back through there tonight and collect more supplies from the horses. In the morning we send the horses back to the cabin with the girl. We get a look at the UAV's pictures before daylight and get on the trail."

But at 1:00 AM the UAV showed no human heat sources for miles, except their own.

***

By the time Sue joined her family at the river, they had, with the help of Tony's labor, dragged the raft to the water's edge. A full moon provided some light. Sue's teeth flashed in a grin.

"Thanks for not killing him, Pa."

"Maybe you don't want to thank me. He's married. That matter to you?"

"He's the first fella to come calling. I can't be picky like city girls. Besides, he's awful cute."

"We'll keep him around, then."

"What's his name? Can't keep calling him blondie."

"She says his name's Tony. Her brother."

"Well, that's good, Pa. Shows he takes care of his kin, just like we do. Does he have any babies?"

"Three."

She rubbed the inside of Tony's thigh. "My. My. I love babies. Let's see how fast we can make you a pa again."

"That'll have to wait. We need to leave these parts. Caleb, you got those ropes tied off."

"Yeah, Pa."

"Sue, keep that gun on your boyfriend while we lever the raft into the water." The raft slid into the river with a small splash. "Get Seth on board." Sue and Caleb carried Seth onto the raft. "Now the in-laws. You two lay down. Don't want you washing off with your hands tied. Caleb, take the rudder. We got a good time of year for this. Shouldn't have to steer round many rocks."

This time they let Tony lay next to Christi. Her ploy had worked. She whispered.

"Thanks for coming for us."

"Sorry I didn't do a better job."

"That's okay. You rescued Terri. At least someone in our family will survive. My parents are dead, aren't they."

"Yes. I'm sorry."

"We knew they were. Jacob said he wouldn't hurt them if we cooperated, but he had blood on him when he caught up with us."

Tony kissed her forehead. "I was working with the FBI. They'll find us. We just need to keep praying and look for chances to help ourselves."

The raft jolted against a rock, and Christi gripped his coat. From that point they had no more opportunities to talk. Jacob had been wrong about the rocks. The raft scraped over the top of many, and nearly knocked them off, jarring into others. Eventually those became fewer as the water deepened downstream.

XI

Tony tried to stay aware of how much time had passed and estimate the speed of the river, to guess how far they traveled. It would only be a guess. When Jacob finally steered the raft into an eddy, Tony knew that they had traveled well over ten miles.

Would even the UAV find them that far out?

Jacob leaned over Tony, who gasped when he felt the knife slice his scalp. "Yeah, that'll bleed real good."

Sue protested. "What'd you do that for?"

"When they find this raft with a lot of blood on it, they'll think we killed him." Christi yelped when he pulled out some of her hair. "I'll stick this in Seth's blood and they'll think we killed 'em both."

"You're so smart, Pa."

Tony felt a little hopeful. Smart, but not twenty-first century smart. Jacob knew nothing about DNA.

Jacob kicked him. "Get up, boy. You got work to do. Help the woman get Seth off."

Jacob and Caleb removed the mooring ropes and rudder from the raft, then Caleb used the rudder to push it back into the river until the current caught it.

They again put Tony to work helping move Seth. Sue led the group up a forty-five degree slope, through trees, to the base of a cliff. She searched for a moment, before pulling branches aside, revealing a darker spot against the dark rock.

Tony's heart sank. *A cave.* The one place the UAV could not find them. He shook his head to fight the hopeless feeling. *Garret can track us to the river and tell that they had a raft. He'll search downstream. I need to buy time, string Sue along till he finds us.*

"Here, girl," Jacob said. "Your boyfriend had a flashlight. Might as well use it till we can get a fire going."

The flashlight briefly illuminated rustic fixtures and furniture. Sue pointed the beam at an armchair, where they sat Seth. She guided Tony to a bench, then pushed him down. He watched as she pointed the flashlight at a fire ring with wood already arranged. Within seconds, flames flickered. Caleb replaced the branches over the entrance.

Tony surveyed the cave. A wall had been built across most of the wide opening, using lodge poles as big around as a man's arm. Smaller branches had been woven through these, providing a fairly solid cover. No one would see light from the fire unless they stood just outside the entrance.

They had built benches, chairs, a table, cabinets. Four stall-like structures along the back of the cave seemed to be bedrooms. Though they were all open in the front, they provided some privacy. That surprised him. Bed rolls hung from wires, out of the reach of rodents. A dozen ammo boxes were stacked against one wall beside empty plastic jugs.

Sue strolled over to Tony and rubbed his chest. "Can I have some fun now, Pa? I think I earned it."

"No!" Then he thought a moment. "Well, wait now. Just a little. We need to see what else he has on him. You could get his clothes off."

Sue giggled. "That's a start. I'll have to untie him."

"Go ahead. Caleb will keep a gun on him. And he won't try anything that might make us hurt his little sister. Give me his coat first."

While he again searched all the pockets, Sue removed the Kevlar vest. Finding no pockets in it, she tossed it aside.

"Give me that, girl." She retrieved it for him. He examined it and read the label. "Kevlar. That's one of them fancy bulletproof vests. Won't weigh you down like the flack jackets we wore in Nam."

"Can I have it, Pa?" Caleb asked. "Sure looks nice."

"Might as well. Might save your life some day."

Sue unsnapped Tony's shirt and pulled it off his shoulders. She threw that to her father, then removed the thermal undershirt. She gasped. "My! Have you ever seen muscles like that?"

She rubbed her hands over his abdominal muscles, then up to his chest, and over his arms. Her body odor effectively removed the slim possibility that he would be turned on by her attention.

Jacob scoffed. "He's skinny. You got to bout starve to show muscles like that. We all got 'em. Just got sense enough to cover 'em with a nice layer of fat."

"I like seeing 'em."

"Quit admiring him. Get on with it."

"He's wearing a necklace. Never seen a fella wear a necklace."

"What's on it?"

"A cross. Like Ma used to wear."

"You can have it. Look better on you."

"I'll get it later."

She unlaced Tony's boots, but her eyes never left the vicinity of his belt buckle. With his boots out of her way, she slid between his legs. He tried to ignore her as she removed his belt and tossed his knife scabbard to her father.

Jacob admired the Native American beadwork. "This ain't something you find in the tourist shops. This is genuine, handmade by a real Indian. You part Indian, boy?"

Tony felt uneasy. *Should I tell the truth? He sounds like it might be a positive thing. Just say as little as possible.* "My great-grandmother was Chippewa."

"Is that right? Who made the scabbard?"

"My great-uncle."

"Nice work. I'll keep that for myself. My granddaddy was Cherokee. Sue, your man is looking better all the time."

"He sure is." She grinned and took her time with his jeans. She eased back, staying on her knees, but prodded him to his feet. She pulled the jeans down around his ankles. He caught his breath as the long underwear followed. She stayed busy.

Caleb chuckled. "You know she's good when she can even turn her own brothers on."

Jacob spit. "It's her teasing started all this fuss. Had to get you boys some women before you knocked up your own sister. Should have left her with your Ma. Girl, you wait with that till later. Give me his jeans."

She pulled Tony down again and finished removing his jeans while he tried to quiet his pounding heart. How long would he have to refuse her advances? How long could he, before she tired of him?

He could only help Christi if he stayed alive. He needed to stay alive for Kelly and the kids. *What am I willing to do to stay alive?*

He jerked when he felt her tongue on his belly. Caleb laughed and wrapped his arm around Christi.

"Give you any ideas, woman?"

Tony's ability to ignore Sue returned. *How can I be turned on by someone who condones kidnaping, rape, and murder? She's as bad as the rest of them.* He felt repulsed by her.

"Sue," Jacob said. "We got work to do. Let him put his long johns on before he catches cold. Then make up your bed. Use these handcuffs on him. I found the key. Christi can bandage his head. After we get all our chores done, you can make your baby. First we got to doctor Seth's leg."

She forced Tony to lay on her bed, then cuffed his hands to a pole that connected the walls. While Christi treated his wound, he examined the pole, finding that it ran the width of the stalls. He could not loosen it without pulling down the whole structure.

Seth screamed, then fell silent.

Jacob spoke. "He'll sleep till morning. Good thing the bullet went right through. Sue, cook us some grub."

"Why can't she do it?"

"We tried eating her cooking. She has a bunch to learn. She ain't been cooking since she was ten, like you have. After supper, you can make your baby. You can even hang up a blanket and have your honeymoon tomorrow. Just like your brothers did."

"Thanks, Pa."

"Anything for my girl. I didn't mean what I said before. You're not a bad girl. Just need a man, like all women do. I should a remembered that when we went after the women for your brothers."

"Glad you didn't, Pa. I like this one."

***

Later, Sue fed Tony and gave him water, before stripping him down to his socks. While she undressed, he heard Caleb raping Christi. He fought back tears, more disinterested than ever.

Sue pounced on him, giggling. Tony found it hard to describe how her attention felt. Annoying? Repulsive? Certainly not exciting. And not for lack of effort on her part. His first time with Kelly, he had thought of her as aggressive. Sue made that encounter seem tame. No. Nothing about this situation put him in the mood. Not even knowing that his life depended on keeping her happy.

She sighed. "What's wrong, honey? I even brushed my teeth for you. Are you shy?"

"I'm sorry. I've had kind of a bad day."

She giggled and crossed her arms on his chest, resting her chin on them. "I guess you have. But you know you have to give me a baby or Pa will kill you."

"I know. That doesn't help. Too much pressure. Then there's my little sister right over there. I'm kind of worried about her."

"Don't be. Caleb's a good husband. Not like Seth. He's stupid. You should feel good bout getting Terri away from him. Think bout that."

"Yeah. That's a good point." Tony sighed. "I just didn't plan on either of my sisters having a husband yet. They're so young."

"They're not so young. Only a couple years younger than me. I thought I'd end up an old maid till I saw you today. I thank my lucky stars that it was me got the drop on you. They'd a killed you for sure."

"Thanks for that. I hope you can be patient with me."

"Well, I'd sure be a lot more patient if you at least acted like you're trying."

"I'm sorry. Guess I'm pretty distracted."

"Well, I got your attention now. You can at least give me a kiss."

Tony did, finding that she had indeed brushed her teeth. He made it last long enough to impress her.

She giggled. "My. My. That really got my juices flowing. What else you got?"

"I'm pretty good with my hands, but I guess that's out of the question."

"Pa don't want to lose any sleep wondering where you are. Caleb has to put hobbles on Christi too. But maybe tomorrow we can get your hands working. You just rest tonight. We don't have to do nothing but make babies tomorrow."

She snuggled in beside him, pulling the bear skin blanket over them. He said a prayer of thanks for finding the right words to buy himself time. But how much longer would his reprieve last?

XII

"This operation is no longer covert. Fly me in a forensics team," Garret ordered over the airwaves. "I want to know everything there is to know about these people. There's a clearing big enough to land a chopper. And keep that UAV up there. They didn't just vanish."

He handed the radio back to his technician and glared into the breaking dawn. He stalked away from the cabin, neatly divided into four little rooms, with four beds. They had missed someone, a fourth member of this twisted family. That person had not gone to the Fisher ranch with the others. Tony would have seen a fourth set of tracks.

When they saw two bad guys drag the deer off, then another started shooting at them, they thought they had accounted for everyone. But the other one—the little guy—ambushed Tony. They had followed Tony's tracks all the way to the cabin, where they disappeared on solid rock.

He felt grateful that they had not killed Tony, but could not understand their reasons. Tony had wounded one of them, judging by the blood and the lack of a body. *What do they stand to gain by keeping him alive?* Maybe they saw him as a harmless hostage. But whether he was a threat or not meant nothing to these animals. *It doesn't make sense.*

"Thank God they had a reason to keep him alive, whatever it was," he muttered to himself.

He walked around the cabin, trying not to think about how he would break this news to Kelly. Of course, they could find no tracks. The cabin had been built on solid granite. That rock ended just past the right side of the cabin, but extended to the left as far as he could see.

"They must have gone this way."

He motioned for his subordinates to follow and traversed the rock, shortening his stride when it became wet. The rock ended just beyond a waterfall. He moved away from the cliff, finding better footing off the granite.

He waded across the stream that flowed from the waterfall and ordered the others to search its banks while he looked at the end of the rock slab. Even he could track on soft, wet gravel. He saw nothing bigger than a raccoon track.

"Why walk across rock with dangerous footing when you'll just have to leave tracks in another hundred yards?" He surveyed the area. "But they didn't leave tracks. I must be wrong about this."

The only other way to go without leaving tracks was up the rock face. Tony could have done it. But he had doubts about the Fisher girl. And what about the wounded man?

He returned to the slippery surface, this time hugging the wall. As he edged closer to the waterfall, he saw the void behind it. He moved in, wondering if he could actually walk behind the cascading water. It sounded like something that only happened in the movies.

Garret checked his footing. When he raised his eyes to advance, they locked on a spot chest high. About a foot of moss had been scraped off with no time to start growing back.

"Good man, Tony." He turned and yelled. "Over here! By the waterfall!"

Four of his men came on the run.

"One of you, wait here and brief the rest. There's a void behind this waterfall. See this mark. Tony left it for us."

Garret ignored their skeptical expressions and pulled his gun, keeping it pointed down as he passed behind the water. He ducked under the overhang, obviously not big enough to hide six people.

When he emerged, he felt behind the vines. Solid rock. More solid rock. Then nothing. He pulled the vines aside, revealing the crevice.

"The back door. I want five guys with me." He pointed. "You, go back and get two more. Catch up to us. We're burning daylight."

He forged through the vines, stopped long enough to pick up the broken vine, then rushed up the crevice. He finally slowed when he neared the far end, mindful of a trap. Finding himself in the clear, he searched for tracks.

Tony's boots and a small pair of athletic shoes left distinct marks. Several sets of moccasins had left vague tracks. And someone had half-carried the wounded man, still leaving blood behind.

The other men caught up.

"Tony and the Fisher girl are leaving an easy trail. The guy Tony wounded is leaving a blood trail. We should all be able to follow that."

Garret led them up the slope at a jog, then scrambled down the other side. Going downhill they found few distinct tracks, but many places where feet had slid on the steep surface. The slope leveled out near the river. Reaching the water's edge, he could read the signs.

Broken branches surrounded parallel skid marks into the river. Deeper footprints indicated that several people, including Tony, had exerted themselves. A pool of blood had gathered where the wounded man sat during the operation.

"They put a raft in the water, then waited. I guess for their sniper. What's the name of this river?"

Someone checked a map. "The Broken Arrow, sir."

"Tell that UAV to search downstream. A long way downstream. Let's get back to the canyon."

XIII

"Before she turns you loose," Jacob said. "I want something clear. Maybe you could kill her with your bare hands. Don't even think about threatening us with that. I'll let you. She picked you. Folks got to be responsible for their decisions. Then I'll make you watch your sister die before I kill you. Understand?"

Tony nodded. "Yes, sir."

"Go ahead, girl. Then give me the key and the cuffs." He pointed at Tony. "I want to hear her moaning."

He left the cubical, dropping the blanket into place. Tony could follow that order. He knew how to make a woman moan without his full participation. He spent the next half-hour showing Sue a good time. But when she caught her breath, she scowled at him.

She kept her voice low. "That was real fun. At least I know you're trying. But that ain't going to give me a baby."

"I'm sorry. I *am* trying. Can you settle for just enjoying yourself for a while longer?"

She giggled. "Didn't know a man would be willing to do that. Pleasure a woman without getting satisfied himself."

"I'm trying to stay alive here. I do that by keeping you happy. But I've never done this with someone I don't know at all. I've never done it with this little privacy. There's never been so much pressure. I'm not at my best."

She nodded, her brow furrowed. "Pa can scare the living daylights out of a person. He's threatened to kill all of us at one time or other. And meant it." She caressed his cheek. "So I'll give you some time to work up to it. I'll see if I can talk him into a more private place. Till then, you'd better pleasure me some more."

He managed to exhaust her. As she slept in his arms, he knew that he had bought himself more time. *How long will she be willing to wait?* His request for privacy might get him outside. He had to give the UAV a chance to see him.

The family seemed to know nothing about Unmanned Aerial Vehicles. The more often any of them left the cave, the more chances that they would be spotted by the UAV.

***

"A woman?" Garret said to the lead crime scene investigator. "You think the fourth unsub's a woman?"

"We'll have to wait for DNA confirmation, but I'd bet on it. We found long hair, a mirror, and evidence that this person is no more than five feet, six inches and one hundred thirty pounds."

"They took Tony for the same reason they took the Fisher girls."

"What's that?"

"Sex."

"Oh."

"Is your team ready to go?"

"We've collected everything we could."

"I'm going back with you. I have to be the one to break this news to Tony's wife."

The twenty minute flight to Spruce Lake seemed surreal after days spent on horseback traveling to and from this site. As the helicopter landed by the sheriff's office, Ryan waited nearby. When he saw Garret, he looked behind him.

"Where's Tony?"

"Captured."

"What! How?"

"Give me a ride over to park headquarters. I'll tell you when I tell

Kelly."

"Is he alive?"

"Yeah. And he's smart enough to stay alive."

"Why wouldn't they kill him?"

"The same reason they didn't kill the Fisher girls."

Ryan stopped with the door of his vehicle open. "But ..."

"There are three men and a woman."

"You're guessing."

"Get in. It's the only thing that makes sense. I couldn't figure out why they didn't kill him. He shot one of them. He helped Terri Fisher escape. They had to be pretty ticked off."

Ryan turned the key and shifted into gear. "That situation wouldn't be too tough for anybody but Tony. He takes those commandments pretty seriously."

"Tony's smart enough to stay alive."

"You're not telling Kelly about that."

"I don't want to. I won't if I don't have to. But Kelly has a way of prying things out of you. I won't lie to her if she comes right out and asks."

"Pray she doesn't ask."

"Amen."

Ryan stopped in front of the headquarters building, and they both entered. Kelly smiled when she saw them, but also looked beyond for Tony.

Her smile faded. "Where's Tony?"

Garret guided her toward Don's office. "He's been captured."

"Good God," Don said.

Kelly sank into a chair. "He's dead."

"No, Kelly." Garret kneeled in front of her. "We were able to track him for quite a while. If they were going to kill him, they would have done it right away. They needed him alive."

"Why? Why would they need him?"

"He helped Terri Fisher escape. They probably figured it wouldn't hurt to have another hostage."

"Oh. How will you find them without Tony?"

"We have that UAV drone up there. You can even read a license plate off those pictures."

"But it can't see anything if they're in a cave."

"Tony's smart. He knows about the UAV. They can't stay in the cave all the time. He'll figure out a way to talk them into letting him out."

"Yeah. He's smart. How will I tell the kids?"

"Lois and I will help you," Don said. "And you just keep praying. Tony's not alone out there. Remember that."

Kelly nodded. She looked at Garret. "He's not even wounded?"

"No sign of blood at all. Not even hurt. Walking like always."

"I'll pray. Thanks for telling me yourself. It would have been harder to hear second or third hand."

"I'm sorry, Kelly. I feel like I let him down."

"I know you did the best you could. So did Tony."

***

"You're a pretty girl," Tony said, caressing Sue. "I'll bet you clean up good."

She smiled. "No, I'm not."

He kissed her. "I know a pretty girl when I see one. If you got a bath and trimmed up your hair a little, you'd put those city girls to shame."

He could not really see in the dim light of the cave, but her expression suggested that she blushed.

"You sure got a silver tongue."

"A woman needs to hear compliments."

"I like taking a bath. Kind a tough in the winter. But I can take one here."

"Maybe we both could. I need one too."

"I'll check with Pa. He don't want you getting away."

"Tell him I won't go anywhere without my sister. You know how important my family is to me."

She left the cubical, just wrapping a blanket around herself. He listened to the discussion.

"Pa, I want to take Tony down to the spring for a bath."

"What for?"

"Cause I want one. And he'd smell nice for me."

"Was this your idea or his?"

"I like to taste my man. I want him to taste good."

Caleb laughed. "She's got a wicked tongue, Pa."

"Shut up. Okay. You can go if you take him and Christi along. He's pretty rank too."

"Thanks, Pa."

"I know you want his hands loose. So put a leash on him. Tie a rope round his neck and tie him to a tree. He can still do what you need him to."

"Yes, Pa."

She pulled the blanket away from the cubical opening and handed Tony his boots.

"How about my clothes?"

"Don't need them for a bath."

"Isn't it kind of cold to go out naked?"

She giggled. "You can take a blanket. Then we got to put the cuffs on till we get to the spring."

Tony laced up his boots, feeling a small sense of satisfaction. Four bodies outside for the UAV to see. Every little bit would help.

After Sue cuffed his hands, she collected a gunny sack and a coil of rope and led the way. Christi followed her, and Caleb brought up the rear with his rifle on Tony. Sue stayed close to the rock face, keeping away from the river, but moving upstream. Tony paid attention to his surroundings, filing the information away for future use.

Thick pine trees screened the cliffs from the river. If Garret had found their escape route and followed them down river, he would pass by without seeing anything.

The scent of pine hung in the moist air. He could feel that they walked on a thin layer of organic matter, mostly pine needles, over rock. The trail descended gradually into a bowl filled with steaming water. It seemed like an unusual location for a hot spring.

"Sit," Caleb said.

Tony obeyed. Caleb handed Sue his rifle and took the rope. He tied one end around Tony's neck and the other to a small tree growing out of a crack in the rock ten feet from the pool. Then he retrieved the weapon and placed it well out of Tony's reach.

Sue giggled and brought the key to the handcuffs. Tony noticed Christi look from him to the rifle. Almost imperceptibly, he shook his head. He needed a plan before they tried to escape, one that put Christi in the least possible danger.

"Get your boots off," Sue said. "I got soap and shampoo. Pa always brings some when he goes for supplies."

When Tony slid into the water, he found it about body temperature. This pool must lay some distance from the hot spring that fed it. But it felt good.

He told Sue that. "Thanks."

"Oh, you know how to thank me."

"Let's start by washing you. Ever had a man give you a bath?"

She just giggled. Tony thought about the water temperature while he entertained her. If the UAV took pictures while they were here, it would only see a hot spring. But still, they had to travel to and from the spring. This seemed to be his best bet for detection. He had to motivate Sue to take a bath every day.

After he washed her hair, she took the bar of soap and began working on him.

"Come on, woman," Caleb said. "I'm ready for you."

Christi obeyed, climbing astride him. Tony turned his head away and clenched his fists. He had never felt so helpless.

Sue saw the tears in his eyes and caressed his cheek. "That really hurts you, don't it."

"She's my little sister."

"It was kind a rough on her at first. But she got used to it. She don't mind it now. That Terri was another story. Don't think she would a made it. Not as tough as Christi. You got the right one out a here. You're a good brother."

"Thanks. But seeing Christi with your brother just doesn't do anything to put me in the mood. Can you understand?"

She nodded. "Caleb, you bout done over there?"

"For now."

"Get lost."

"Huh?"

"Tony can't get started with his little sister around."

Caleb sneered. "City boy."

"Well, this city boy's all I got. Now, get!"

"I go back to the cave without you and Pa'll have my hide."

"So don't go back. Get an armload a kindling. That'll give us enough time. Won't it, Tony?"

He smiled. "Better make it a big armload." *I can fool the rest of them if I keep her entertained enough to play along.*

Sue blushed. "You heard the man, get lost."

While Caleb and Christi dressed, Tony kissed Sue's neck, making her shriek. After they departed, he kissed her forehead.

"It might not happen this time, but I'll guarantee that you'll have the best time of your life today. You won't even mind that there'll be no chance for a baby."

She grinned. "Prove it."

Tony made her hyperventilate until her eyes squinted and she rubbed her temples.

Mission accomplished. "Oh, I gave you a headache. I'm sorry. That can happen when you get too excited. Just take deep breathes and try to relax. Here, let me do that for you."

"Man, I never had a headache like that. I was having a great time till that happened."

"I was trying so hard to give you the time of your life, I forgot about that. Next time, I'll stop and let you relax for awhile, then we'll do some more."

"It's getting better." She opened her eyes. "Just give me a couple minutes, then you can do some more."

He kissed her forehead. "I like your enthusiasm."

After two more sessions of foreplay with a rest break between, she sat leaning against him.

"You proved it."

"You're happy?"

"Oh, yeah. You can take some time getting around to the baby-making."

"Thank you. We can call this courting. Most couples have time to get to know each other before they start making babies."

"Guess I don't know nothing bout that. Guess my brothers didn't know either. Pa should a told them."

Tony bit his lip. "Your Pa wouldn't like it if he knew we weren't trying to make a baby, would he?"

"Oh, no. He wouldn't like it at all. Maybe he don't know about the stuff you do. Maybe that's why Ma divorced him."

"Maybe. This will have to be our little secret then. But that means you have to get him to give us time alone. Do you think you can talk him into that?"

"You bet I can. He knows you won't try nothing long as Christi's at the cave."

"You can have it as often as you can get me alone."

She grinned up at him. "You're good at this courting stuff."

Caleb emerged from the trees. "He get it done yet?"

"He about wore me out."

"Huh. Didn't think he had it in him. Get going."

Tony had to help Sue from the water, then steadied her.

She smiled. "You sure do know what you're doing."

***

When they reached the cave, they found Jacob and Seth sitting by the fire, drinking coffee. Seth appeared pale.

Sue ignored him. "Pa, I picked me a good one."

"Well, I was starting to wonder if he could finish what he started."

"Aw, Pa, he's just shy. He was a rich kid that always had his own room. He done good when I got him alone."

"Alone?"

"I told Caleb and Christi to take a walk. He was still tied up. If you kept her here, I could take him out all the time. He won't go nowhere without her."

Jacob spit into the fire. "He'd put a bullet in all a us if he had the chance."

Tony smiled slightly. "In a heartbeat." He meant it. "But I won't do anything to endanger Christi."

"Why would a man admit his weakness?"

"You already know my weakness. I love my sisters."

Jacob laughed. "That's so. Well, if Sue gets knocked up, she'll settle down. That'll make life easier for all a us. Boy, you remember what I said? We won't even put cuffs on you when you go out. If you do anything stupid, your sister will pay for it."

"Yes, sir."

"And, Sue, you keep him away from the river. I'll go down there from time-to-time looking for tracks. If I see that you've been down there, I'll whip you both. And Christi. You understand, boy?"

"Yes, sir."

XIV

Garret and Ryan stood over the table covered with the UAV's pictures. Ryan rubbed his mustache.

"Nothing?"

"All kinds of things. Deer. Elk. Bear. Even a hot spring. No people. Not for five miles on either side of the river. Not till you get close to the town of Broken Arrow. It's like they just vanished."

"There's cliffs on both sides of the river for twenty miles. They're loaded with caves. They must be holed up in one of those."

"Lot of good that does us. We can't search dozens of caves. And my bosses are going to take the UAV away from me. The military is complaining about these daily flights."

"We can't give up. Tony's still out there."

"I don't intend to. I've talked them into letting me float down the river tomorrow. And I've talked the military into taking one training flight a week over the area. I'm not leaving here till I find Tony."

"They'll let you keep working on it?"

"When they tell me to stop, I'll use my vacation. I'll take a leave of absence if I have to. If I don't find Tony before they run out of patience, I'll resign. I owe him that."

"If this becomes unofficial, let me know. I have a bunch of vacation coming."

"Thanks, Sheriff."

"And if you need any help, all you have to do is ask. Tony has a lot of friends. We've turned a bunch of them away more than once. They want to do more than going to a prayer service and helping Kelly."

"I wish throwing a lot of people at this would help. But we'd just get somebody else killed. If I end up on my own, I may need them for support staff."

"Whatever they can do. Horses. Supplies. Transportation. And that includes aircraft." He sighed. "Anything helpful from the crime lab?"

"Lots of DNA for future reference. Not many good surfaces for prints. No hits on the ones we found."

"Did Terri Fisher ever come around enough to tell you anything?"

"Yeah. After they sedated her some. The kidnappers are a family. The father, Jacob. Two sons and a daughter, Seth, Caleb, and Sue. The sons started raping the girls the first night after they were kidnaped. Considered them their wives. Evidently this Sue is some piece of work too. They kidnaped the girls because she was teasing her brothers so bad that their father was worried about incest."

"That's what saved Tony."

"I handed him to them on a silver platter."

"Quit beating yourself up. That doesn't do Tony any good. One of you had to provide cover. And I'd bet he's a whole lot better with a rifle."

"Yeah. You still believe that he's alive?"

"Yes. Don't you?"

"Yeah." He shrugged. "I've just had too much experience with kidnapers. They usually kill their hostages after things go sour."

"These aren't your run of the mill kidnapers. They didn't want ransom. They didn't want to make a statement. They wanted sex. And if that woman was willing to go after her brothers, Tony's wedding ring won't bother her a bit."

Garret nodded. "Keep reminding me of that."

"Have you had to tell Kelly about it?"

"No. But I'm supposed to go over there in a little while. I may have to give her a reason to keep hoping."

"You know his parents are there?"

"I heard."

"You find out any more about that family?"

"Only one person had any face-to-face contact with them. Way out west, but probably twenty miles from their camp. They traded pelts for ammunition, coffee, first aid supplies, and occasional luxuries. The guy only saw Jacob and Caleb. They'd come one day, tell him what they had and what they wanted. He'd go to town and get it. They came back the next day. Never had any problems with them."

"How long?"

"He said about ten years. The first two years only Jacob came. This guy thought Caleb was fifteen or sixteen when he first saw him. We have another report of a sighting a couple years ago. Guy thought he saw bears till he put his scope on them. Two men in bear skin coats. The rest of the reports are all missing livestock or property in very remote areas. These people kept a low profile till now."

***

When Garret walked up to the kitchen door, Tony's father opened it before he could knock.

"Agent Garret."

"Mr. Wagner. I ... I'm sorry just doesn't cut it."

"No, it doesn't. But not because it's your fault. Come in. Is there anything new?"

Garret entered, finding Kelly and Tony's mother sitting at the kitchen table. Kelly shifted Justin in her lap. Garret's mind flashed back to that night, less than two weeks before, when Tony sat in the same chair holding the baby.

Kelly had dark circles under her eyes.

Garret let his breath out. "Not much. We've learned a little more about the kidnapers, but nothing very helpful."

"I want to know," Kelly said, her words very precise. "Why you think that they wouldn't kill him once they were safely away?"

Garret sighed and Tony's father pulled out a chair for him. Garret took it.

"Maybe you don't think he's still alive," Mike Wagner said.

"Yeah. I do. And I even think he's safe for the foreseeable future. But ... it's going to be awfully tough for him."

"Tell us what you know." Kelly again used the carefully controlled words.

"The kidnapers are a father, two sons, and a daughter. All adults. They kidnaped the Fisher girls as wives for the sons. When they captured Tony, I think the daughter decided it was her turn. Nobody can think of any other reason they didn't kill him on the spot."

The room fell silent. Tony's parents looked at Kelly. Her expression told them nothing. Finally, a tear rolled down her cheek. Her words came with more emotion.

"And if he doesn't put out?"

"They wouldn't keep him around.   And he knows that. "

Kelly wiped the tear away, then placed Justin's bottle on the table. "They still have Christi Fisher. He knows that he's her best chance. He won't let her down. Tony will stick around to take care of her."

Garret noticed how the statement had carefully avoided any reference to sex or murder.

"That's what I thought. I want to get both of them out of there as quick as possible, and for the same reason. And I know Tony will be watching for chances too. He won't take unnecessary risks with that girl."

After a few more questions, Mike walked Garret to his car. His voice quivered. "Tony will do what he needs to stay alive. But he'll be devastated. He's tried so hard to lead a godly life. He'll think that he should have let them kill him."

"I know. And so does Kelly. He won't see that he's being raped, just like the Fisher girl. He'll think that he had a choice. Sex or death is no choice."

XV

The next day, Tony found a place downstream, but near the cliffs, to entertain Sue. He picked the spot to give him a view of the river, filing the information he collected for use during his escape.

After she caught her breath, they headed back to the cave. When he saw rapid movement ahead, he touched her arm and froze. Caleb appeared at a dead run, making a hand signal that Tony did not understand.

Sue did. She pivoted toward him.

"What ... ?"

She clamped her hand over his mouth and shouldered him back. He yielded, especially when Caleb reached them and used the business end of his rifle to encourage him. Tony's back hit the rock face.

"Not a sound," Caleb hissed.

He and Sue crouched beside Tony. Sue removed her hand, believing that the muzzle of the rifle under Tony's chin provided enough motivation to keep him quiet. But she gripped his arm.

He could see the river through occasional breaks in the trees. Then something yellow. A raft! He succeeded in not letting his excitement show.

The raft came to shore, downstream from the cave. Tony had noticed that the family only retrieved water from one boulder below the cave. The searchers would find no tracks.

"See any tracks in the mud?" a very familiar voice asked.

Garret! If I yell, Caleb will pull the trigger and they'll find Christi. But the brother and sister both saw his reaction. Caleb pushed the muzzle harder against his jaw.

Sue clamped her had over Tony's mouth and whispered. "You pull that trigger and they'll be all over us."

Caleb nodded, switching the rifle to his left hand. He pulled his hunting knife and placed it against Tony's throat. "You try anything, they'll never hear you."

"Nothing here," an unfamiliar voice said.

"Okay." Garret sounded discouraged. "Push off."

The raft disappeared from view. Tony felt defeated. He had held out for the UAV and Garret. If the UAV had seen anything, Garret would have made a covert approach. He had no idea where they were.

Tony's legs began to shake and tears ran down his cheeks.

Caleb spoke, still whispering. "See that, Sue. He don't want to be with you. He was hoping they'd find him."

"Caleb, sometimes you can be the backside of a mule." She wiped Tony's tears. "A course he wants to go home to his kids. Ask Pa how tough it is being away from your kids."

"I reckon. Follow them. Make sure they keep going. I'll get him back home and trussed up."

She nodded and jogged downstream. Caleb released Tony and let him feel the knife against his back. When they reached the cave, he whispered again.

"Pa."

Jacob only pulled aside enough of the cover to let them slip in, then closed it behind them. Seth clamped the handcuffs on Tony's wrists, tight enough to bite into his skin, then shoved him down on a bench.

"Any trouble?" Jacob asked.

"Naw. He was sensible. But they came to the bank. We heard 'em talking. He knew one a 'em."

"That right, Tony?"

"Yeah. A good friend of mine."

"They letting your friends come look for you?"

"He's in law enforcement. A lot of my friends are."

"Not smart enough to know you can't do much tracking from a boat. But smart enough to find our back door. It's early. Doubt they'll camp close enough to be a bother. Sue'll keep an eye on 'em. Don't see any reason why we should lose sleep."

Tony tried to control his emotions, but when he saw Christi crying, he failed. He channeled the emotion into anger.

"These cuffs are cutting my wrists. Nobody else puts them on this tight."

"Shut up," Seth said.

Jacob glanced at Tony's wrists and saw the blood. He tossed the key to Seth. "Don't need to be that tight to hold him."

"Pa, why you coddling him?"

Jacob backhanded him. "Do like you're told. The man shot you cause you're too stupid to find proper cover. You got no call to carry a grudge. He could a killed you."

Seth followed orders with hate in his eyes. Tony met his gaze. Seth posed the greatest danger to him. When he fully recovered from his wound, Tony would need to watch his back.

Seth limped to the other side of the cave and Christi eased her way to Tony's side. He looped his arms around her and held her while she cried.

"What you crying for, woman?" Caleb said. "This is your home now. You don't need nothing from those folks."

Tony wished he could hit Caleb. Instead, he kissed Christi's forehead.

Jacob spoke, almost gently. "Leave her be. She ain't been with us that long. She still misses all her fine city things."

When Christi's tears subsided, she pressed her mouth close to Tony's ear. "I think I'm pregnant."

He stiffened, then hugged her, then thought of Sue. *How much longer can I put her off?* He began saying the Lord's Prayer just loud enough for Christi to hear. She joined him, then, for the first time in days, smiled.

XVI

"I gave you a week," Sue said. "And you've made courting fun. But it's time."

Tony sat in the cave with one wrist handcuffed to a chain, giving him just enough slack to sit outside of Sue's cubicle. The men had gone fishing, leaving him alone with her and Christi.

He hung his head. *I could overpower her and even break free of this chain. But I don't have a plan. If Christi and I take off running, they'll track us down. Probably kill both of us.*

Sue continued. "I've been patient, cause I knew you needed time. But I got an itch that needs scratching. If I tell Pa that you ain't been scratching it, he'll beat me. But he'll kill you. So get your clothes off and let's do it. Christi can wait outside."

"Let me talk to him," Christi said. "Maybe I can help him."

"Well, now. That sounds like a fine idea. I'll give you a little room."

She stepped outside. Christi sat on the bench beside Tony and hugged him.

He looked up with tears in his eyes and whispered. "I was supposed to rescue you. I'm sorry I messed it up."

"No. It didn't go as planned. But it means so much to me that you're here. I felt hopeless before I saw you. Even when I got Terri loose, I didn't think she could make it. She's safe, thanks to you. It's like a weight's lifted off me."

"I don't think I can do this."

She squeezed him. "You have no choice."

"Yes, I do."

She sat back to stare at him. "They'll kill you if you don't hook up with her." His jaw set. "That's what you're talking about." She began crying. "I need you alive. You have to survive. If you don't, I can't. Please do it for me."

Tony gazed at her and his body relaxed. *I would be deserting her.* He nodded and wiped her tears and his own.

"Okay. I'll keep working on a plan to get away. When I see the opening, you'll know."

She kissed his cheek. "I couldn't ask for a better brother." She left the cave and Sue returned, grinning.

"Get your clothes off."

Tony took a deep breath, channeling his anger and frustration. "You, get them off."

She laughed and obeyed.

He tried not to think, focusing on her skilled efforts to stimulate him. It worked. Within minutes, he shoved her down on the bed. He kept his eyes on the cave wall until he finished. Then he sat beside her, staring straight ahead.

He felt ill. When she snuggled up to him, his stomach churned even more. He swallowed again and again. Any woman would take offense if a man threw up after having sex with her. And this woman would probably have him killed for it.

He finally gained control of his stomach, then fought tears. He wrapped his arms around her and held her close, not letting her see.

She heaved a contented sigh. "That was worth waiting for. You done good."

He stroked her hair. *What have I done? I'm willing to compromise my beliefs just to stay alive?* He shook his head. *I did it for Christi. I have to remember that.*

    ***

As Tony suspected, Sue had a ravenous appetite. He convinced her that he needed some time between sessions. *Sessions.* He could deal with it better by thinking of it as a session rather than sex.

At least twice a day, she escorted him away from the cave. He preferred the spring. The warm water seemed to make her foreplay more effective and it could all be over faster. Though his stomach felt queasy afterward, it was never as bad as the first time.

He got better at thinking about other things so that her hands and lips on his body would not repulse him. His body could do the job without much help from his brain anyhow. When he began gasping, it signaled his mind to return.

Autopilot. I use autopilot for the sessions. I can be planning our escape while she uses my body. He half-smiled and kissed Sue's forehead. "You're pretty good at this."

She let her fingers trail down the center of his chest. "I had lots of practice. But my brothers were never the challenge that you are."

"They're younger. Men get to be more of a challenge as they get older."

"How old are you?"

"Almost thirty-two."

"You're quite a lot older than Christi and Terri."

"Yeah." He quoted the lie Christi had told. "Mom was just a teenager when she had me. That's why she gave me up for adoption."

"Pa couldn't give us up. That's why he came back for us when we were old enough to pull our own weight."

"How long have you lived with him?"

"Since I was twelve, so about seven years. He took the boys a year before. He told me that he wanted Ma to teach me more about woman stuff. But he came back like he promised."

"Do you ever miss the city things?"

"I used to. Then I'd remember how the other kids treated me in school. I never belonged there."

"Tell me about your pa. He's not from around here is he?"

"Arkansas. We left there before I can remember. Pa needed a place with less folks around. He thought a cabin in the mountains would do the trick. But he just plain don't like folks."

"Thanks for sharing this stuff with me. It makes me feel more like part of the family."

She reached under the water to caress his thighs. "You give me a baby and Pa will consider you part of the family. How about another try?"

"It's pretty quick. But I'll see what I can do."

XVII

Garret stared at the dark stains on the raft. The crime scene investigator had already lit it up with luminol. Blood. While the woman collected samples, he struggled against the worst case scenario.

Tony and Christi are dead. He shook his head, trying to banish the thought. *Tony wounded one of them. This is probably his blood.*

"There are long, blond hairs stuck in this stain," the CSI said.

Garret bit his lip. "Can you test for blood type right here?"

"Yeah. As soon as I get everything collected. Do you know their blood types?"

"Memorized them."

He hopped off the raft and took a walk along the shoreline. Fishermen had found it a mile upstream from Broken Arrow, caught on a snag. The only new evidence in days. But the raft only told him that the Brock family had gotten off somewhere in the twenty odd miles upstream.

DNA collected from their abandoned camp had led him to a seven-year-old child abduction case. He had spoken to Rachel Brock, a mother who had lived in the same cabin all that time, hoping that her children would tire of the mountains and come back to her.

She told how Jacob had left them more than a dozen years ago. But he returned each summer to visit his children and bring bundles of furs for her to sell. He would even take the boys—and Sue when she was old enough—camping for a week. Later longer.

But he always brought them back when he promised. One morning she would wake up to find him gone. Then, eight years ago, she found Caleb and Seth gone too. Sue had assured her that they wanted to go.

"Agent Garret." He looked up. "This one is O positive."

Tony's blood type. *Along with about half of the world's population. Get a grip.* He returned to study the stain while she tested the other.

Jacob Brock likes to stab people. That isn't near enough blood for a stab wound to the chest.

The CSI caught his attention again. "This is AB negative."

"The Fisher girl is O negative. That's from Seth Brock."

"You think the hair was planted?"

"If we think they're dead, we might not look so hard. Put a rush on that O positive DNA. But it looks to me like they might have beat Tony up a little. That isn't life-threatening blood loss."

***

Garret questioned people around Broken Arrow, but nobody had seen anything suspicious. The next day, he returned to Spruce Lake. When he walked into the sheriff's office, Ryan looked hopeful.

Garret shook his head. "It only helps because my superiors will keep me on the case awhile longer. We already figured they got off the river sometime before Broken Arrow."

"Nothing else?"

"Some of Tony's blood. I just got a DNA match. Not enough to make me think they killed him. They might have beat him up some. Or they could have cut him hoping we would think he's dead."

"What do you plan to tell Kelly?"

"Just that we found the raft. Though I might make it sound more encouraging than it is."

"Can't we scour those riverbanks? I could get you plenty of volunteers."

"The thought's crossed my mind. But we really don't want amateurs finding these people. We'd just get someone else killed."

Ryan sighed and leaned back in his chair. "I just keep thinking about Tony and Christi. And unwanted babies."

"Yeah."

"How's Terri doing, by the way?"

"A lot better. She should be coming back here any day now to live with a foster family. She's had a lot of counseling. And it helps that she didn't get pregnant."

"Thank God for that."

XVIII

While Tony caught his breath he noticed for the first time that he had no nausea. *I must be getting used to this.* Guilt washed over him and the nausea returned.

Sue rubbed his chest, but he avoided looking at her. Then he saw Jacob, leaning against a tree, watching them. That neither shocked nor scared Tony. He even smiled.

"Do I pass inspection?"

Sue turned, surprised. "Hi, Pa. Well, does he?"

"Just wanted to make sure he was doing his job and you weren't covering for him."

"Now why would I do a fool thing like that?"

"Because women in love do fool things. Guess the only fool thing you're doing is taking a bath twice a day."

"Not every day." She splashed water on Tony. "But he makes it worth it."

Jacob spit. "I got work to do."

He walked away and Tony gave her a long kiss. "That sounds like a good idea."

"What?"

"Work. Put me to work. I'm getting soft."

She giggled and caressed him. "No, you're not."

"You want me to keep these muscles you like so much? Put me to work."

"If we fetch firewood on the way back, Pa'll see that you want to help. Maybe he'll give you some more chores."

"Okay. Let's go."

"But you only take what you can carry. Pa gets real mad if we drag anything back."

"Your pa's a pretty smart man, isn't he."

"You bet. Nobody gets the drop on Pa. He hates stupid. He might a beat Seth half to death if you hadn't shot him. He figures you taught him a lesson."

"Did I? I don't trust him."

She laughed. "But you trust the rest a us?"

"I know where I stand with you. If I do as I'm told, you'll treat me fairly. You won't double-cross me. I think Seth would stick a knife between my ribs if he had the chance."

"He does and I'll kill him."

Tony finished lacing his boots and kissed her. "That'll be a great comfort to me when I'm dead."

"I'll watch your back."

"Now that makes me feel better."

***

"Why would you want to help us?" Jacob asked from his chair by the fire.

"He's just trying to get on your good side, Pa," Seth said. "Don't trust him."

"You think I'm stupid enough to trust him? When you start pulling your weight, I might listen to your jaw flapping. Till then, keep it shut."

Tony waited until he was sure that Jacob had finished. "Christi's working, why shouldn't I? I'm used to work. When Sue isn't keeping me busy, I'm tied up. I don't much like that."

Jacob smiled. "Thought you'd give me some flowery speech bout pulling your weight. Being chained don't set right with a man. Had my doubts if you qualified for a while. But you're one a those men that don't pound his chest."

Tony thought he might actually have earned Jacob's respect. "If you walk the walk, people will know you're a man."

"Seth, you hear that? Ain't that what I been telling you?" Seth just glared at Tony. "We'll give you chores. Same arrangement. Your sister stays here when you're out and Sue goes along."

"Thank you, sir."

"Get to work, then. Take some jugs down to the river and get water. Sue, make sure he don't leave tracks."

Tony hid his elation as he gathered the jugs. He had wanted to get back to the river. It seemed to be his best avenue for escape. Chores would give him many chances to learn the lay of the land. He followed Sue, feeling good for the first time in, how long had it been?

Long enough for him to grow a full beard. He had never tried it, so was not sure how long that had taken. He had no idea what day it was. They tended to run together with no job to go to, no schedule to keep.

He needed some way to keep track of time. Only one thing stood out. He remembered exactly how many times he had been with Sue.

That thought dampened his mood, but not for long. He would use that quirk to keep track of the days. Nine days. And he had been captured a week before that. More than two weeks since he had seen Kelly and his kids. How much longer would it be?

He shook his head. Those thoughts accomplished nothing. He had to concentrate on planning their escape. He and Sue reached the river.

Sue hooked her fingers into his jeans. "I think Pa likes you."

"Well, that's good."

"Course he'd still kill you if he had to."

"That's what I'd expect of him."

"You wanting to work sure gets my juices flowing."

Tony lay the jugs aside. "Just about everything gets your juices flowing."

She giggled and unzipped his jeans. Tony switched to autopilot.

***

Over the next two weeks, Tony familiarized himself with the land between the cliffs and the river for a mile on either side of the cave, even stretching that distance a little farther downstream. Sue sometimes questioned his excursions. They could find firewood closer. But he learned that he could silence her doubts by promising special sexual favors when they reached a place up ahead.

Jacob quit demanding to know what had kept them so long after Sue replied with giggles a few times.

Sometimes Tony stayed closer to the cave, planning his route, leaving tracks along the river as often as he could. Sue did nothing to stop him.

The river had dropped and the current slowed in the time since their arrival. It would also warm steadily as less of the water came from snow melt. But he knew that the river would never be warm enough to safely spend much time in.

He stopped and rocked a log laying along the shore. He grinned. "You think I can carry that one back to the cave?"

Sue laughed. "No. But I bet you can lift it."

"Let's see."

He seized one end, bent his knees, and lifted it with some effort three feet off the mud. He returned it to the same spot. That and another, twenty yards downstream would serve his purpose.

Sue wrapped her arms around him. "I like seeing your muscles bulge."

"I know. That's why I lifted it for you," he lied.

"I thought Caleb was a pretty good husband to Christi, but you put him to shame. You're always doing nice things."

Tony laughed. "Nobody's threatened to kill him."

"That the only reason you do it?"

"No. I like seeing you happy."

It surprised him how easy it had become to lie. He gave Sue a long kiss to keep her from thinking too much about it.

She smiled. "You got over being shy too."

"You get used to things. It helps that your pa's giving me more freedom. I'm just not in the mood when I'm chained up."

"So still no fun at night. Pa wants to sleep."

"Don't blame him. I wouldn't trust me either."

"I don't trust Seth. Since he's feeling better, I think he's laying for you."

"I know. I'm keeping my eye on him."

"I told Pa bout it. He thinks you can take care a yourself."

"I can, in a fair fight. But I'm unarmed."

"I'll stick to you. Told you I'd watch your back."

"Thanks."

Tony now recognized the real danger he faced from Seth. Jacob's reasoning may have worked if Seth wanted to get even for Tony wounding him.

But Tony had noticed Seth's expression one day when Sue hung on him. Jealousy, rather than revenge, drove his hatred. The sick pervert had lost Terri and once again had his eye on his own sister. Tony stood in his way.

XIX

Kelly stood over the kitchen sink, fingering her wedding ring. She stared at the window with tears running down her cheeks. Medication had ended her sleepless nights. So she found these times toughest.

Brett and Christina had gone to play with friends. She had put Justin down for a nap. The quiet house gave her too much time to think.

The doorbell offered welcome relief. She wiped her eyes on her way to the door, not recognizing the woman outside of her new house. Probably at least forty, wearing jeans and a western shirt, she smiled when Kelly opened the door.

"Mrs. Wagner?"

"Yes."

"I'm Emily Garret. I believe you know my husband."

"Oh." Her brow furrowed. "Yes. This is a surprise."

"Well, he isn't coming home. I thought I might as well come here. He won't leave till he finds your husband."

"Please, come in. Does that surprise you?"

"No. He was a Marine. Or, is a Marine. They don't say it in the past tense. Never leave a man behind. Besides, he thinks the world of Tony."

"I know. I'm just afraid that the FBI will tell him to quit looking."

"Don't worry about that. They've given him another week to work on this, then he'll take accumulated leave time, because he *will not* leave."

"That means so much to me. But how do you feel about it?" Kelly gestured to a chair and Emily took it.

"Wyatt calls very few people his friends. To them, he is intensely loyal. I love that about him. Many of his friends, I barely know. But I feel like I know Tony. Wyatt always has stories to tell after he works with Tony."

"I think they hit it off as soon as he decided that Tony wasn't a serial killer. Though they seem to have very little in common."

"They're detectives. Their minds work alike." Emily shifted in her chair. "I came to see my husband, but he's busy most of the time. I thought perhaps I could do something to help you. It would mean so much to me."

"Thank you. People seem to think I should take time off work. But that would just give me more time to think about what Tony's going through. At first, I had more help than I knew what to do with. But as time's passed, less people offer. The ladies from church take turns helping me clean and do laundry. It keeps me from feeling overwhelmed. Most of the time."

"Do you get to take any time for yourself?"

"What's that? Tony used to make me go soak in the tub once in awhile. Or give me a night out with my friends." Kelly bit her lip. "Your husband won't let me give up hope. He says that woman will keep him alive. But it's hard to keep believing that."

Emily took her hand. "I don't know as much about this case as you do. But if he didn't believe it, he wouldn't say it. Wyatt's a skeptical man. He must be convinced that Tony's alive."

"You're right. He's pretty hard to convince. I guess it's reassuring, when I think about it that way. Would you like some coffee?"

"Only if you'll let me make it."

"Oh. I suppose. Everything is right above the coffee maker. What *do* you know about what happened to Tony?"

"A couple was murdered, their teenaged daughters kidnaped. When Wyatt heard that Tony was working the case, he asked for it. They followed the girls' trail back into the mountains, got lost in a blizzard, came home, then went out with more men. They found one of the girls but, in the process, Tony disappeared."

"Just what's in the newspapers. I'll tell you the rest."

"You don't need to. If it will be hard for you."

"Everybody thinks I shouldn't want to talk about this. I need to talk about it."

"Okay."

Kelly proceeded to tell her everything she knew about Tony's kidnaping. Emily poured coffee, then left it to get cold in her cup. She asked no questions until Kelly finished.

"Wyatt calls Tony 'the reverend'."

"Do you know why?"

"He was a seminary student?"

"Yes."

"So he probably never slept around?"

"He can count the number of women he's been with on one hand."

"What he's going through would be easier for a guy who's a dog. He'd probably just see this as an inconvenience. I don't see Tony taking it that lightly."

"Tony will feel that he should have let them kill him, rather than break that commandment. I want him to come home, no matter how many commandments he has to break."

"He'll need that kind of support when he gets home. He's lucky to have you."

"I'm the one who's lucky. Thank you so much for coming, Emily. You're just what I needed."

XX

Tony sat on the bluff overlooking the river, with Sue's head on his thigh. Their clothes lay under them. They both enjoyed the warmth of the summer sunshine. He stroked her hair to keep her quiet while he scanned the opposite river bank.

Like the north side of the river, cliffs lined most of the south side. Pine and aspen grew on the slopes between the river and the cliffs. In places, they thinned to almost nothing, while in others they completely blocked the view of the cliffs from the river.

Caves pocked the base of the cliffs on that side too. He could see one from here. Wide and shallow, like most of the others.

They had formed when the ground underneath eroded, taking away support for the rock. It collapsed from its own weight. Chunks of this rock cluttered the entrances and floors of all but the oldest caves.

When he and Christi escaped, they would float down the river as far as they could stand the cold water, then get out on the opposite bank. They would walk downstream until they reached civilization, seeking shelter in caves hidden by trees.

Sue stretched and sat up. "It's real pretty up here."

"Yes, it is."

"I always liked this home better than any a the others. Never much liked going so long without a bath. Could take a bath here year round. But the game ain't so good in the winter. Pa said we'd starve to death here."

"So where are we going this winter? Back to the other place?"

"Can't do that. The law knows bout that place. No. We got a couple more scattered round the country. Nice and snug."

"Where?"

"Pa would beat me if I told you."

"I suppose. Your pa doesn't like taking chances. I'll bet he thought long and hard before he went after my sisters."

"You can count on that. He just got real mad one day and told the boys he'd get them some wives. Kind of made me mad that he didn't think bout me."

"He had to prioritize."

"What's that mean?"

"He had to deal with his worst problem first. That was Seth."

"Suppose. Seth's a different one. Don't know why he can't get over you shooting him. Don't make no sense."

"That's not why he hates me."

"It ain't?"

"Seth is jealous. He wants you for himself."

Sue laughed, but her eyes betrayed her concern. "I'm his sister. That'd be sick."

"It is. He is."

"No. Can't be."

"I've watched his eyes when you and I are together. I'm right about this."

Sue gazed at the river for some time. "Maybe. When we was younger, we took baths together. And we figured out that I could make them feel good and they could do the same for me. Seth was real happy to do that. Told Caleb he didn't have to. Pa even gave him a whipping and told him to keep his hands off me. That's when Pa said he'd get them some wives. Is that why Pa took that chance?"

"Yes. He was afraid that Seth would do more than make you feel good."

Sue shuddered. "But he's *my brother*. He couldn't think that I'd want that."

"Would he care if you wanted it?"

Sue nodded. "Cause he knows I'd kill him if he did anything that made me mad."

"Then he probably thinks that you want it. He's probably convinced himself that you're only with me for the same reason he was with Terri. So you won't get in trouble with your Pa. He's infatuated with you. He probably thinks that you feel the same."

"What's that mean?"

"Ah-h. He has a crush on you. He thinks he's in love with you."

"He really *is* sick." She bit her lip. "And dangerous."

"I know. Since Terri's gone, he's frustrated. That makes him even more dangerous."

"He won't try nothing with Pa around."

"I figured that. That's why I like to stay out in the open like this when we're together. I don't want him to surprise me."

"Pa said you was smart. You can outsmart Seth."

"I hope so."

***

Every time Tony found something to like about one of his captors, he reminded himself of how he had found Jill and Blake Fisher. Or he looked at Christi. He would not allow himself to fall victim to the Stockholm Syndrome.

Jacob was a rapist and cold-blooded killer. Caleb daily raped a seventeen-year-old girl. Sue saw nothing wrong with their behavior, or with kidnaping him. Tony did not have to worry about liking Seth. That would never happen.

Within the cave, they allowed Tony to move freely between Sue's cubical and a bench against the wall farthest from the door. He rubbed his wrists, chafed all night by the handcuffs, as he watched Sue cook breakfast.

Jacob and Seth drank coffee by the fire.

Only Sue's cubical had a blanket covering the opening, so they all saw Caleb rise. He grinned while he poured coffee. "I'm letting her sleep this morning. I think she's knocked up."

"Thought she been looking kind a peaked lately," Jacob said. "Your Ma was real sick with you. Let her rest and leave her be. Don't want her losing that baby."

"How long I got to do that?"

"Give her a couple weeks. She'll feel better. What you think bout being an uncle, Tony?"

Tony shrugged. "I still think she's too young."

"You still ain't given Sue a baby."

"I have three kids. So you know I can do it. But it usually takes me a while. Up to six months one time."

Caleb and Seth snickered.

"Shooting blanks," Caleb said.

"Three kids. Just not shooting a machine gun."

Jacob laughed and Sue stopped cooking to caress Tony's thighs.

"Don't care what he's shooting. He has a good aim."

Tony pulled her onto his lap and kissed her while reaching inside her shirt. Sue gasped. He knew that the performance would make Seth boiling mad. Tony had decided to push his buttons, forcing Seth to move against him, rather than waiting for it.

"You don't wear out," Jacob said. "That's for sure. Sue, save that for after we eat."

She finished cooking, and even let Tony eat. Though she returned to the cubical. She came out naked. Caleb laughed. Jacob looked bored. And Seth fumed.

Tony bent over to untie his boots. "Guess chores will have to wait for a while."

She helped him up and removed his jeans. He kissed her as he backed behind the curtain. With the calculated nature of this performance, Tony did not need autopilot. Once inside, he did everything he could to make her as vocal as possible, adding to the chorus himself.

Sue unknowingly contributed the finishing touch by showering him with compliments that could be heard by anyone in the cave.

He doubted that Seth could take much more of this before he exploded. He just hoped that he was prepared for that eventuality.

As Sue lay exhausted in his arms, Tony realized that he had not needed autopilot for some time. He admitted that he looked forward to sex, the only thing that gave him some release from the constant frustration he felt.

He had worked out his escape plan and had daily opportunities to execute it. But he never had the chance to take Christi with him. They were only allowed to leave the cave together with escorts. One or more rifles always separated them.

He had to continue to bide his time and wait for them to make a mistake. He only hoped that when that time came, Christi would be in a condition to make the formidable run. He had told her that he had a plan in place. He had encouraged her to eat and exercise to keep her strength up for the journey. But he doubted she could do that with morning sickness.

He thought about sex again and felt the old wave of nausea. He extracted his arm from under Sue and sat up.

"Where you going?"

"You just rest a while longer. I'll get dressed."

He left the cubical, grinning at the men. The hate he saw in Seth's eyes sent a chill up his spine. He would not have to wait much longer.

Tony pulled on his jeans, then sat to put his boots on, trying to think of something to say that would goad Seth without irritating Jacob. But Seth vented first.

"It's not right, Pa. You never let us screw around all day. Why you let him get away with that? He's not pulling his weight."

"Shut up. He's bout gathered 'nough wood for next winter. He fetches water and goes fishing. What else can he do? Want to give him a rifle so he can hunt? Sides, I ain't had no trouble with your sister since he come. Never seen her so happy. I got two happy kids and one that would gripe if you hung him with a new rope."

Seth stormed out of the cave to Caleb's amusement. He grinned at Tony. "He sure don't like you."

"I noticed."

"Just riles him that you're getting some and he ain't."

Jacob poured the last of the coffee into his cup. "That boy'll be the death a me."

XXI

"Are you sure you want to do this?" Garret said, suitcase in hand.

Kelly smiled. "Yes. You're putting your own time into finding Tony. You shouldn't have to spend money on a motel. I have a spare bedroom. Having you and Emily around can only help me."

"Okay. If you're sure."

"Will you need room to work?"

"No. Ryan gives me office space."

He carried the suitcases to the spare bedroom while Emily made coffee. When he returned to the kitchen, he took Justin from the high chair. Kelly began cleaning up the remnants of Justin's cereal.

"What *are* you doing to find Tony now?"

"As much as I can. But I'll admit, it isn't much. I've been out to visit the guy who these people trade with. He knows how important it is to contact Ryan's office if he hears from them. I checked with him again yesterday. He still hasn't seen them and they're past due."

"Any idea why?"

"They may just think it's a good idea to lay low. But we found a lot of pelts at their camp. They may have nothing to trade."

"Do you think they'll come back for them?"

"No. We have a hidden camera with a satellite link and a motion sensor pointed at the cabin door. It's transmitted twice. Both times we caught a bear on camera. I spend a lot of time pouring over the latest pictures from the UAV, looking for heat sources. Looking for any changes that might be manmade. And I go through the case file, trying to find something that I might have missed."

Kelly pulled him down to kiss his forehead. "Thank you. I know you're doing the best you can."

"Am I? I want to hike down that river and scour both banks. Search from cave to cave. I'd bet they're holed up along the river, where they can get away fast again if they need to."

"That would take an army. Two armies. Because you'd need one on both banks. You need a place to start. Sooner or later one of them will be out of the cave when that UAV flies over. Then the Bureau will give you all the backup you need."

"I don't want you to have to wait that long. Tony's been missing two months. I don't want Tony to have to wait that long. He's counting on me to do everything humanly possible."

"You just said it. You can't do the impossible. How much leave time do you have?"

"Nine weeks."

"That will take you to the end of the summer. That will be enough time."
***

But Tony had long since quit counting on anyone but himself. He no longer prayed for someone to find him. He only prayed for the wits and the strength to seize the opportunity to escape with Christi when he found it.

He followed Sue along the now familiar trail to the spring. Today, he watched her undress.

"What you waiting for?"

"Just enjoying the view. I was right. You do clean up good."

She looked at her reflection in the water. "I like having my hair trimmed up. Christi did a nice job."

"I think she felt better after you cut her hair too."

"You're right. She even smiled. She don't do that much."

Tony stripped and pulled her against him. "I appreciate you doing something nice for my sister. To show my appreciation, we'll do whatever you want today."

She licked her lips. "You know how I like it."

He did and he gave it to her, for a very long time. Her screams echoed in the little hollow. But they would not be heard at any distance due to the sound of the river. They rested and swam for a half hour, then, feeling especially frustrated, he came again. She smiled up at him, rubbing his chest.

"My! That don't happen much."

"Do more nice things for Christi and you'll be surprised how grateful I can be."

"I'll see about it."

They climbed out of the water and dried themselves on the warm rock before dressing. Tony had just put his boots on when he saw Seth. He touched Sue's arm. She stood, wearing only her pants.

"What you doing here?"

"I got as much call to be here as you do." He swaggered over.

"You spying on us?"

"Spying? The law'll find us for sure if you keep yelling like a whore."

She slapped him. If she saw the blow coming, she did not try to avoid it. He punched her in the jaw, sending her flying. She lay on the rock, stunned.

Tony landed a blow to Seth's mid section, and another to his jaw, making him stagger backward. Tony glanced at Sue, noticed her moving, then gave Seth his full attention.

Seth shook his head and pulled the large hunting knife he carried. Tony kept his eyes on it. He had seen Seth throw it with deadly accuracy. But Seth would keep it in his hand if he thought that Tony could dodge the missile and take possession of it.

Tony knew that he had to stay on his feet and follow every movement of the knife to survive.

Seth wiped blood from his mouth. "By the time I finish with you, you won't have nothing left she wants."

He lunged. Tony eluded him three times, then landed a blow. Seth changed his technique, slashing rather than lunging. They moved around the rock enough to allow Tony to see Sue push herself to a sitting position.

She screamed. "No!"

Tony jumped back, but Seth kept coming. The knife sliced across Tony's right forearm. He spun and shoved Seth in the back. Seth fought to stay on his feet, giving Tony time to regroup. Sue screamed for Jacob.

"Shut up!" Seth came at Tony again, slashing the air with short strokes. He advanced while Tony continued to retreat. "Coward!"

"Sooner or later, you'll wear out. I can keep this up longer than you can."

Tony hoped to get him enraged enough to throw the knife. Instead, Seth charged him, trying to use his bulk to knock him over.

Tony seized the wrist holding the knife with his left hand, twisted to the left, and planted his right fist in Seth's mid section. Seth did not double over, but he bent forward, struggling for air.

Tony wrenched the knife from his hand and plunged it between Seth's shoulder blades. He pulled it out and backed away.

He would never forget Seth's shocked expression. He gasped, coughed up blood, and fell on his face. Blood quickly spread across the back of his shirt. Tony retreated a few more steps, still holding the knife.

"Drop it, boy," Jacob said quietly.

Tony obeyed. His head cleared and he focused on Jacob's rifle.

After all I've done to survive, it can't end like this. Lord, don't let it end like this. Executed for defending himself. He felt thoroughly defeated.

"Pa, it's not Tony's fault. Seth was crazy."

"I know." Jacob kicked Seth's body. "He saved me the trouble. Told you he could take care of himself."

Tony sank to his knees and buried his face in his bloody hands, sobbing.

***

When Christi saw Tony covered in blood, she became hysterical. Sue hugged her and reassured her while Jacob guided Tony to his bench.

"Most a that blood ain't his. He's just got a little cut. Help me doctor it up."

"Where's Seth?" Caleb asked.

Jacob spit into the fire. "Dead. And good riddance."

"What happened?"

"He pulled a knife on Tony. Thing is, that's all the knife Tony needed."

"He killed Seth?"

"That's a dumb question."

Caleb ran his hands through his hair. "And you don't care?"

"Course I care. Saved me a bullet. Your brother's been asking to get killed since he let his woman get loose. Maybe before that. I just been waiting to see if Tony had the sand to do the job for me."

Their voices sounded far away to Tony. He leaned back against the cave wall, exhausted. Sue bandaged his arm while Christi washed the blood off of him. He gazed at Christi and his mind began to clear.

When they finished, Jacob offered him a cup. "Drink this."

Out of habit, Tony obeyed. He choked on the whiskey.

Jacob smiled. "You back with us?"

"Yeah."

"Never killed a man before?"

"No."

"First one's the toughest. You bawled. Me, I threw up. Vietnam. You get used to it."

"I didn't cry because I killed him. I cried because you didn't kill me."

"Now why would I do a fool thing like that? We got Seth's chores to divide up. Make more work for us if I killed you. No. I think I made a pretty fair trade, you for Seth. I got two good sons now, two good daughters, and a grand baby on the way. Life's good. You rest up a bit, then you and Caleb can go bury him."

XXII

Tony and Caleb carried Seth's body to a shallow cave and piled rocks on it. Tony kept a cautious eye on Caleb. Unlike Jacob, he grieved for his brother. Tony would have worried more, but Jacob made his son leave his weapons in the cave, just like Sue did when she went out with Tony.

Instead of returning home, Caleb walked down to the river. Tony followed, because he always followed whoever he was with. But when Caleb sat on a boulder near the water's edge, Tony wondered if he would like to be alone.

"Want me to go back?"

"No. I'd just have to explain that to Pa. But thanks."

Tony sat on another rock and left him to his thoughts. He felt relieved, knowing that he had eliminated the greatest threat to his life. He felt no remorse for killing Seth. But he felt bad for Caleb. The brothers must have been close.

Caleb sighed. "You should a known Seth when he was a kid. Pa liked him back then. But he changed when Sue started looking like a woman. We always took baths together. And it was her idea that she wash us and we wash her. Don't get me wrong. I liked it as much as she did. But Seth, he did all kinds of extra things for her. Even told me he loved her. Told me he wanted to make a baby with her. It wasn't natural and I told Pa."

He sighed and Tony waited for him to continue.

"Pa beat him. Told him to leave Sue alone and he'd find a woman for him. You know the rest. Don't know if things would a been different if Terri hadn't got away. But seeing you with Sue just drove him crazy." He shook his head. "I didn't help. I ribbed him about it when Pa wasn't around. Never thought he'd try to kill you."

"I did."

"Yeah? You were waiting for it?"

"I knew he'd do it sooner or later."

"Guess Pa's right. You're smart. Better get back before he thinks you killed me too."

"Now *that* would be a fool thing to do."

***

Tony saw the knife and fought against the handcuffs. But he could not get free. He screamed as it penetrated his chest.

"Tony, wake up! It's just a nightmare."

He woke, gasping, with Sue sitting beside him. He looked down at his chest. "Oh, God."

"The same nightmare?"

He nodded several times. "Get the key."

"You're safe. Nobody's going to hurt you."

"*Please,* get the key. I need to get up."

"Okay."

By the time she returned, his breathing had slowed, but his heart still pounded. When he left the cubicle, he found Jacob stirring the fire.

He dropped to a bench nearby and tried to steady his shaking hands. "I'm sorry, sir."

"Not your fault. Even dead, that boy's a thorn in my side. I had nightmares for years after Nam. Didn't get rid of them till I moved out here."

"The handcuffs make it worse. When I try to defend myself, they become part of the nightmare."

"Imagine they would. Your wrists are bleeding again. Let's try rigging something up round your ankle with that length of chain. Sue, give me those cuffs, then doctor his wrists."

Jacob used one of the cuffs like a padlock, holding one end of the chain around Tony's ankle. He fastened the second cuff to the other end of the chain, after passing that through the frame of the cubicle.

Tony lay back and tried to relax.

Sue snuggled into his arms and whispered. "This is better for both a us."

"Yeah."

"Seth sure messed you up. Glad you killed him."

He let his breath out. "I'm not. I wish I hadn't needed to."

"You're a kind man, Tony. After what he put you through, you still feel that way."

"I guess so." He yawned. "I'm *so* tired."

"Try to sleep. Maybe this will help with the nightmares."

"I'm afraid to sleep."

"You got to try."

"Okay."

The nightmare returned. But this time, when he tried to fend off the knife, he woke sitting up, gasping. No screaming. He only disturbed Sue. Afterward, he relaxed much faster.

> ***

Over the next week, the nightmares decreased in frequency and intensity. Tony quit dreading sleep.

Sue sat in the cubicle beside him and placed his hand on her belly. "There's your baby."

Tony tried. He fought to control his emotions. But tears escaped. Sue's smile faded.

"Aren't you happy?"

He wiped the tears away and told another lie. "I'm sorry. You just made me think about my kids. I try not to do that. I miss them."

She hugged him. "Oh, I understand. Pa lived out here for a long time before he came back for us. He came and visited every summer, but he just missed us so much. Some day, you'll see your kids again. When all the excitement dies down. Till then, you'll have this one to love."

Tony hugged her, feeling absolute defeat once again. For the first time, he felt like he wanted to die.

"Come on, now. Get dressed. I want to tell Pa."

They dressed and, as they left the cave, Tony noticed rifles sitting against the wall. They did not even worry about keeping him away from the weapons anymore. *They think I'm completely whipped.* He never considered picking up one of the rifles and using it against them.

The rest of the family sat outside in the morning sun. Sue wrapped her arm around Tony. "Tony gave me a baby."

Jacob and Caleb celebrated. Christi tried to meet Tony's gaze, but his eyes dropped.

Jacob noticed. "What's wrong? You look like you lost your last friend."

"He just misses his kids, Pa."

Jacob nodded. "Yeah. New baby'll make you think bout the others."

"Can I talk to him?" Christi said. "I think I can help him."

"Inside."

She took Tony's hand and led him into the cave. "This has nothing to do with your kids. I know just what you're feeling because I felt it too. I just wanted to die."

Tony hugged her and they cried together. "I should have let them kill me."

"No. No. Remember, you're my hope."

"But I'm not doing you any good. They won't leave us alone, unguarded. I need to get you out of here before you're too far along."

"They're starting to trust you. Look at the guns. They think they've beaten you. Don't make them right. Don't give up. If you give up, then I do too. You're keeping me alive."

He nodded. "I'm sorry. I lost it there for a while. I won't give up. I'll hold it together for you. I'll get you out of here."

"Soon. They'll give us our chance soon."

"Yeah. Soon." He kissed her forehead and they walked outside. "I'm sorry. It's just tough being away from my kids."

"No need to explain," Jacob said. "Now, I got another surprise for ya. We're all getting pretty sick a fish. You can go hunting with Caleb. Help him carry back what he shoots."

The thought of a long hike lifted Tony's spirits a little. He always felt better after exercise. He waited for Caleb to retrieve his rifle, then followed him upstream about a mile. Here, dirt had filled in ancient rock slides creating a slope that reached to the top of the cliffs. The trees thinned on this slope, leaving ideal grazing for deer and elk.

Tony pointed to tracks of both, as well as bear. Caleb nodded and whispered.

"All fresh, too. Don't know bout you, but I only eat greasy bear when I'm starving. Let's find something else."

"Good idea."

"Go on. I want to see you track."

Tony followed the deer, knowing that would be the easiest carcass for the two of them to carry. Deer also proved to be easy to find. In a clearing, they spotted three bucks in velvet, two young and one with a huge rack. With the area too remote for other hunters, these had little fear of humans.

Caleb took careful aim and fired only once, dropping a young buck. The other two disappeared into the trees.

"Nice shot," Tony said.

"You get good when you starve if you miss." They walked to the deer and Caleb poked it with the rifle. "You know why I didn't shoot the king of the mountain?"

"Tough and gamey. This one will be better eating."

"You're not a city boy, are you."

"By your standards, everyone else is a city boy. I was raised on a farm."

Caleb looked from Tony to the deer, and back again. Then he handed Tony the rifle. "Keep an eye out for that bear while I gut him."

The rifle in Tony's hands felt alien. He had a gun. What should he do with it? *Watch for the bear.* The fresh venison would be good for Christi. He stayed alert while Caleb worked. He finished gutting and cut a slit between the tendons and the bones of the front legs. He passed a stick through these holes and tied a rope between the stick and the antlers, already hardened under the velvet.

Tony thought about what the antlers meant. Probably early August. He had been here three months.

He heard the bear before he saw it. The black bear broke from cover, then rose on its hind legs, trying to intimidate them away from the carcass. Tony also only needed one shot to drop it.

Caleb laughed and took the rifle from him. "Pa'll likely beat me when I tell him. But you done good. I don't care. We'll come back for his hide."

They draped the ends of the rope over their shoulders and leaned into their load.

XXIII

Garret fumbled for the cell phone on the night stand without opening his eyes. Finally, he found it and placed it to his ear.

"Yeah."

"Agent Garret?"

"Yeah."

"Captain Reilly. We have human heat signatures."

Garret sat up, fully awake. "When can I see the pictures?"

"On their way to Spruce Lake as we speak. They should reach the sheriff's office about sunrise."

"Give me a general idea where you found them."

"Along the river. Not far from the hot spring."

"Thanks, Reilly. I owe you one big favor." He disconnected and turned on the light.

Emily rolled over. "Wyatt?"

"The UAV found him."

She sat up. "How can you be sure?"

"No one else would be in that area. I'm going down to the sheriff's office. Don't tell Kelly just yet. Let me collect more information."

"What do I tell her when she asks where you are?"

"Tell her I couldn't sleep. I should be able to give her something more concrete by noon."

***

"What's that beside them?" Ryan asked.

Garret smiled. "You haven't spent as many hours pouring over these pictures as I have. That, my friend, is a deer carcass. Freshly killed, by the looks of it. The heat hasn't started to fade yet."

"What's this over here?"

"That's a bear."

"Smelled blood. Hope it ate one of those S-O-Bs."

"That would help our cause. Let's take a look at the normal light picture."

He sorted through the pictures until he found the one taken at exactly the same time as the infrared shot. He had finally gotten over being amazed by the detail that could be seen from that altitude.

Ryan had not. "Am I wrong? Am I seeing that one of those guys doesn't have a shirt on?" Garret used a magnifying lens. After a moment, he sat back and stared at Ryan. "What is it?"

"You're right. He doesn't have a shirt on. And he's blond."

"Tony. Nobody described these guys as blond?"

"No. Black hair. Now I really have something to tell Kelly. But first, I need to call in my team. We'll need logistical support from some of those friends you mentioned."

"Just tell me what to do. And don't think you're going in there without me."

"It's out of your jurisdiction."

"Call me a guide. I can't track like Tony, but I'm pretty fair."

"It'll be good to have you along. While I call Washington, see about an outfitter to supply rafts and provisions for twenty men for a week. We'll find him sooner, but I'm not taking any chances."

Ryan left to make the call in his office. When Garret finished his call, he followed. Ryan thanked the person on the phone and disconnected.

"He'll start putting the stuff together right now. I just told him that it was another search for Tony, but that we didn't have a lot of time."

"Good. We don't want to get everyone's hopes up. The team will be here tomorrow. If you and I can do the planning today, we should be able to leave the next day."

"You *are* going to tell Kelly about that picture, aren't you."

"She needs to see a picture of her husband alive. She deserves it. I'm going down there now. I just need to remind her that he's not out of the woods yet. No pun intended."

"We all need to remind ourselves of that."

***

But try as he might, Garret could not contain his good mood. They had waited too long for any lead on Tony's whereabouts. He burst into park headquarters with a grin on his face. Everyone noticed and anticipated good news.

Kelly put her hand to her chest. "You found him."

"Would you like to see a picture?"

"Of Tony?"

"Taken from 10,000 feet or so."

He lay the picture on her desk, glad that it did not show the bear like the infrared picture. Don and the rest of the rangers looked over her shoulder.

"What am I seeing?"

"Tony and another man beside a deer carcass."

"How can you tell it's Tony?" Garret let her use the magnifying lens.

"Blond hair. Terri Fisher described that whole family as having black hair. It's Tony all right."

"It couldn't be someone else hunting deer out of season?"

"The area's too remote. Anyone who came up river to do some poaching would have done their hunting long before they reached this spot. It's Tony."

"It's Tony." She caressed the picture as tears rolled down her cheeks. "When was this taken?"

"Yesterday morning."

"Now what?"

"We go in and get him. My team will be here tomorrow. If all goes well, we'll leave the next day. Don't get me wrong. There's still danger. But now we're sure he's alive. And we can finally do something besides sit on our hands."

"God hasn't kept him safe this long to let him die now."

"That's what I believe. Now, as tough as this may be, I don't want this information to leave the room. For the kids sake. As far as any of you know, we're just going on another search for Tony. You don't know what we're basing that search on. Got it?"

Everyone nodded, but Don pointed out a flaw in the plan.

"You think anybody's going to buy that, when you go from a one-man search party to an army?"

"I don't care if they do. There'll be a buzz. People will get their hopes up. But it's better if they don't know too much too soon."

Kelly wiped her tears away, but more came. "When you see him, give him my love."

***

"Do you think ten miles is far enough upstream so they won't hear the helicopters?" Garret asked Ryan.

"There are some twists in the river. As long as they take this route in and out." He tapped the map. "These people shouldn't be out hunting. That deer will last them awhile. They should have everything they need close to their cave."

"If only we knew where that was."

"We can make a pretty good guess. There's plenty of game in the area. I'd say it's a sure thing they didn't cross the river." He scratched out the south river bank. "They're probably hunting within a mile of home." He placed black marks a mile on either side of the hunting site. "And look what's a half mile downstream from where they shot the deer."

"The hot spring."

Ryan circled the half mile on either side of the hot spring. "That's where I'd look for them."

"Makes sense. After we fly in, we'll wait till late in the afternoon and take the river to this point." He indicated a spot three miles upstream from the spring. "Just in case you're wrong. Half of us will work our way along the cliffs, checking out caves, until it's too dark. Just before dawn, the other half will float down river to the hunting site, while the first group continues in the same direction. If we don't find them upstream from the hunting site, we'll track from there. I imagine they had to drag that deer back to camp."

"And when we find them?"

"We have silencers. We take out as many of them as we can before they know what hit them. We look for the chance to get Tony and Christi out of there before the shooting starts. We do not let them get to their back door under any circumstances. And we have that UAV in the air just before dawn."

XXIV

"But I could help," Tony said.

Jacob passed the handcuffs through the loop in the length of chain tethering Tony to a boulder.

"I know you want to help. And it's not that we don't trust you. There's just some things you and Christi don't need to know. One of 'em is where we got our back door." He held out the cuffs and Tony gave him his wrists. "Sue can help us work on it. You and Christi sit here in the sun. I know we don't hobble you much no more, but we don't want you getting no foolish ideas."

"I wouldn't."

"Best be safe. We'll be back in no time. Then Sue can make this up to you."

Tony waited until they disappeared downstream along the cliff before he began circling his right wrist, twisting the chain that connected the handcuffs.

Christi watched him for a moment. Her eyes widened. "Should we pound it with a rock?"

"No. They'd hear."

"What can I do?"

Tony kept twisting as the handcuffs bit into his wrists. "Stuff your pockets with jerky. It's not completely dry, but it's better than nothing. Then grab that coil of rope out of the cave."

"That's all? No gun?"

"They took all the guns."

Christi hurried to do as he said, then watched him grimace while he continued to work the bloody handcuffs. They snapped apart and the chain holding him fell away.

He grabbed her hand and ran downhill as fast as he thought she could manage. They slid in places and once he had to catch her before she fell.

When they reached the river bank, he released her and ran downstream to his first log. He worked it into the water, lifting first one end, then the other, until it floated.

"Get me the end of that rope."

He pushed the log downstream until he reached the second log. He held out his hand and Christi gave him the rope. He tied it around the first log.

"Don't let that float away."

Then he worked the other log into the water in the same manner. When it floated free, he shoved it against the first log and took the rope from Christi, wrapping it around both until he used it all. He tied it off.

"Let's go."

As they waded in, pushing their raft, they heard a shout from near the cave. It sounded like Caleb.

"We'll stay in the water, on the far side of this, as long as we can. In case they start shooting. Hang on to that branch."

Christi nodded. When the water reached his chest, the current began pulling the logs. Tony pushed off, trying to send them farther from shore. He changed his mind about clinging to the far side, staying on the end of the logs to use his body as a rudder.

He heard a thump as a bullet hit one of the logs. Looking back, he saw Caleb and Jacob on the shore, their rifles aimed at him. Another bullet hit the water, then another, farther behind. Jacob, then Caleb, lowered their rifles.

Tony said a prayer of thanks. They were safe for the moment.

He worked his way up the log, on the opposite side from Christi. She could not hang on much longer. "You're coming up. Take my hand."

With all the strength he could muster, he heaved her on top of the logs.

"Don't put your arms or legs in between. Just lay across the top."

He worked his way back, again playing rudder, and finding greater success without Christi hanging off the side of the log.

He would have liked to take their little raft all the way down river to the first town, but the cold water prevented that. He began to lose feeling in his hands and feet and his teeth chattered. If he stayed in the water much longer, hypothermia would interfere with his ability to think and eventually kill him.

Using his body, he eased the logs toward the far shore. His knees scraped bottom and he tried to gain his feet. Christi dropped back into the water.

"Are we stopping here?"

Tony nodded. She pulled the logs toward shore, dragging him with her. He managed to give an order.

"G-g-get the r-rope."

He crawled out of the water while she struggled with the wet knots. She pushed the logs back into the current, then helped him to cover. She coiled the rope.

"I'm so cold, but you're freezing."

"We-e have t-t-to keep m-m-moving. T-t-to warm up."

"Okay. I'll help you."

He leaned on her shoulders for about a hundred yards, until his feet began to feel like part of his body again. He took the lead, exhausted, but knowing that he could not stop. He had no comprehension of how much time had passed or how far they had traveled.

"Tony, can we rest?" He did not take another step, dropping where he stood. Christi sat beside him and rubbed his arms and back. "How much farther do we have to go?"

"For what?"

"Before we rest for the night?"

"We can't rest."

"We have to rest. We have to find a place where we can start a fire and dry our clothes."

"We can't start a fire. They'll see it."

"We can look for a cave with lots of trees in front of it. They won't be able to see a fire."

He suddenly pounded his fist on his thigh four times. "My brain isn't working. I got too cold. You're right. We'll look for a cave. But starting a fire without matches is pretty tough."

"Then I guess we'd better use these." She pulled a container from her pocket.

He smiled. "You're an awfully smart girl." He pushed himself to his feet. "Let's go."

They climbed to the base of the cliff and found a cave, but not enough cover. He rejected a second one for the same reason before finding a suitable shelter. A shallow cave with jagged boulders strewn about the entrance and a thick stand of pine trees between it and the river. They began gathering firewood. When they had accumulated a substantial pile, Tony sank to the floor of the cave.

"Can you build it? My hands are shaking too bad."

"Sure. I've gotten pretty good at building fires."

"Put it close enough to some of those rocks so we can lay our clothes on them."

Christi nodded, pulled dry bark from some of the branches, piled twigs on that, then small branches. She struck a match and held it under the tinder until it caught. She added larger branches to her little blaze until it provided life-giving heat.

She draped her jacket over a rock, then took her shoes off and placed them near the fire. She unlaced Tony's boots and did the same.

"Thanks."

"Get your jeans off. We have room to dry about two things. My jacket shouldn't take long. Then we can kind of share that."

She hung his jeans, then decided that she could make room for other clothes by leaning branches against the rocks. Before stripping completely, she removed the soggy venison from her jacket pocket and place in on a split tree limb near the edge of the fire.

Then she huddled beside Tony. He wrapped his arm around her.

"This is better," he said. "My mind isn't so fuzzy."

"Will they come after us?"

"I don't know. And I think I should know."

"If Caleb had his way, he'd come after me."

"Yeah. But Jacob will make the decision. He won't care that both Caleb and Sue want to get us back. I should know what he would do by now, but I just don't."

"Neither do I. What do you think they'll do to us if they catch us?"

"They might slap you around some, but not too bad because of the baby. Me? The best I can hope for is a beating and being chained up forever. But they might kill me. I'd prefer that."

Christi wrapped her arms around his chest and squeezed. "They won't catch us. Do you think anyone is still looking for us?"

"Garret. But what can one man do?"

"Who's Garret?"

"Are you old enough to remember when I was shot?"

"Yeah. That National Park serial killer stuff is the most exciting thing that's ever happened in Spruce Lake. I remember the FBI agents swarming all over town when that guy was murdered in the park."

"Well, Wyatt Garret was the lead FBI agent on the case. He's a friend of mine. I usually work with him when I'm on FBI cases. I was working with him when we found Terri. That day when the search party came down the river, I recognized his voice."

"We probably won't run into a search party. How far do we have to go to find civilization?"

"I'm not sure. If we keep following the river, we'll reach the town of Broken Arrow. I don't remember how far. We should find a ranch before then. Probably a couple of days."

"We can do that. I'd better turn our supper."

She pulled the smouldering limb from the fire, then used a stick to turn the pieces of venison. She did not return it to the fire, letting the hot wood cook it. Tony wrapped his arms around her again.

"I think we should eat all of that tonight. I don't know how good it will keep. There are plenty of berries around now. We'll eat those."

"Okay. When our clothes are dry you can have that shirt they gave me. It's plenty big. I'll wear the jacket. I never understood why they didn't let you wear a shirt."

"I was cold most of the time. Maybe it was another way to control me. I'd want to stay where I could get warm."

"Yeah. Or Sue just liked seeing this body." She rubbed his chest. He shuddered. "I'm sorry. I shouldn't joke about that. I wouldn't like it if you kidded me about Caleb."

"That's okay. Probably do us good to joke about it. What do you plan to do when we get back?"

"You mean, about the baby?"

"Yeah."

"What Caleb did to me was wrong. But I think he would have been a decent guy if he had been raised better. Jacob didn't teach him right from wrong. I can't think of this baby as evil. I want to keep my baby."

"I understand."

"Are you worried about your baby?"

Tony stared at the fire. "It still doesn't seem real. I haven't thought about the baby. Better if I don't."

"I tried that for a while. It didn't work."

"Have you thought at all about where you'll live?"

"I've thought about it, but I don't know. Both our grandfathers are dead and our grandmas live in these one bedroom apartments. Mom was an only child and Dad has one brother, divorced and in the Navy. I just don't know. You think we could live with you?"

"With me?"

"You're my brother, after all."

Tony smiled. "I feel like your brother. There were a lot of times these past few weeks that I found myself thinking of you that way. And I'd have to remind myself that you're not. We're probably closer than most brothers and sisters."

Christi chuckled. "We certainly are now."

He kissed her forehead. "I guess we've gotten pretty used to this casual nudity. I'm not the least bit embarrassed to strip in front of you."

"Me either. But it would be warmer with clothes. I think supper's ready."

They divided the venison and chewed it in silence. When she finished, Christi checked her jacket, pronounced it dry, and draped it over their shoulders.

By the time they lay down to sleep that night, they had a dry shirt and jacket. After some discussion, Christi suggested that he should wear the shirt while she slept closer to the fire. If he "spooned" her, they could drape the jacket over both of them. He consented.

　　While neither of them could claim to be warm, they fended off the cold enough in their state of exhaustion to allow them to sleep.

XXV

When Garret skirted the steaming hot spring, he immediately noticed the well-used trail worn through the pine needles. He pointed to it and used hand signals to split members of his team on either side of the trail. They crept forward, everyone exercising caution to avoid stepping on dry branches.

Although he noted, as an afterthought, that there were very few branches to avoid. Someone had gathered a lot of firewood in this area.

The trail approached the cliff face. When he saw the branches pulled back from the cave opening, his heart sank. He signaled a halt, pressed himself against the cliff, and eased toward the opening. One look inside confirmed his fear. He waved the team forward, but still spoke quietly.

"They're gone. Get that UAV looking for heat signatures. Set up a perimeter. They might not be far. See what you can find out here. Ryan, let's look inside."

Using his flashlight, Ryan kneeled by the fire. "Cold."

Garret shined his beam around.

"I don't think they got wind of us. They didn't leave in as much of a hurry."

"How can you tell?"

"Last time they left behind food, cooking pots, clothes, blankets, a first aid kit, even some ammunition. None of that here. And they couldn't have eaten that deer in three days. They took time to pack."

"But they could be as much as three days ahead of us."

"Probably not. Did you notice the drying racks outside?"

"No. But that's what they are, isn't it. They were drying venison?"

"Let's take a closer look." They returned to daylight and inspected the racks. "Here's some meat stuck to it, not totally dry."

"They left before the meat finished drying. Something spooked them.

Maybe they saw us and figured they had enough time to pack."

Garret swore. He turned on his heel and grilled the technician. "What do you see?"

"Just a minute. I think something's coming up."

Garret called on his headset. "Red team, double time it to our location. The fox is loose."

"There!" the technician said. "Three heat signatures. Straight north of our location. About two miles."

"Three! There should be six!"

The technician watched a moment longer. "No, sir. Just three."

"Can you see them without infrared? Maybe confirm their identities. I want choppers. This is no time to be subtle. We're throwing everything we have at these guys."

While the technician studied the screen, Red Team arrived. Its leader reported to Garret.

"In a cave back there, we smelled decomp. We confirmed that it was coming from under a pile of rocks the right size to cover a body." When he saw the color drain from Garret's face, he rushed on. "In this cool air, it would have had to be there weeks to smell that bad."

Garret relaxed. "It still could have been the girl."

"Oh."

"Send somebody back to at least confirm that it's not the girl." He turned to the technician. "What do you see?"

"There's a lot of trees."

"It's a forest. What did you expect?" He waited.

Finally, the technician smiled. "No blond hair."

Garret faced Ryan. "Three people. No blonds. One dead back there. How do you add that up?"

"Tony escaped?"

"God bless him."

"But we still have to find him. That UAV can't look in two places at once."

"If you were Tony, which way would you go?"

"The easiest way. Downstream."

"Right." He spoke into his radio again. "Bring the boats up." He waved the Red Team leader over. "Arrange a location for the choppers to pick you up. Get those people. Capture them, if possible. But they do not get away. Am I clear?"

"Yes, sir."

"Once you're in the air, you won't need the UAV. It can search down river. With any luck, Tony and the girl will be easy to spot. Tony knows the UAV could be up there. He'll stay out where it can see him. I'll take Ryan and four other men. Use the rest as you see fit."

***

Tony woke and looked around the cave, then lay his head down again. He had been afraid that it was only a dream, that he would wake up chained next to Sue. He reached across Christi and piled more wood on the fire's embers, then snuggled up to her again. She squeezed his arm.

"We're really free."

"Yeah. It will take a while to wake up in the morning believing that. After that fire starts kicking off some heat, we'll get dressed. We don't have much packing to do, just grab the rope and go down to the river for a drink. The sooner we get moving, the sooner we can find something to eat."

"That sounds like a good reason to move."

The cave provided no dirt to smother the fire and they had nothing to carry water in. Tony had to settle for stirring the fire and spreading it out.

Enough distance separated it from anything combustible to make leaving it a negligible risk.

After a drink, they headed downstream, dry clothes and rest giving them a much better outlook. But as the morning wore on, hunger eroded their good mood. Rest stops came closer together. They drank more, trying to fill their empty stomachs.

When the sun stood almost directly overhead, they found a berry patch. Animals had beaten them to it. Tony and Christi devoured every berry they could find. Though the snack failed to satisfy their hunger, it did wonders for their mood.

They moved on at a quicker pace. Before they needed another rest break, Tony stopped so suddenly that Christi ran into him.

"What's wrong?"

He held up his hand to silence her. This time they both heard it. Someone calling his name. Then hers. Too far away to recognize the voice. They looked at each other with fear in their eyes.

He shook his head. "They wouldn't call us. They'd track us down and take us by surprise."

"A search party?"

"Let's get closer to the river. Someplace we can watch without being seen. Just in case I'm wrong."

They scrambled downhill, making too much noise to hear anything until they settled by the river bank. The voice called again, closer.

Tony sank to the ground. "Garret."

"Garret? We're rescued?" Tony did not respond. "Tony, we have to get their attention."

He just sat there. When the raft came into view, Christi took matters into her own hands. She yelled and waved until someone spotted her. The raft eased toward shore. When it neared, the man in the bow shouted to her.

"Is he okay?"

She looked at Tony, who failed to acknowledge their rescuers. "He was, until he recognized your voice."

Garret scowled and jumped into the water when the raft scraped bottom. He kneeled in front of Tony. "Tony, its okay. You're safe. We'll take you home."

Ryan joined him. Tony looked from one to the other, but said nothing. Tears began trickling down his cheeks.

Christi wrapped her arms around him. "Tony, what's wrong? We're safe."

"You're safe," Garret said. "His job's done."

"I don't understand."

"Tony came to get you out. No matter what he went through, he had to stay strong till he accomplished that. He doesn't have to stay strong anymore."

"Will he be okay?"

"I don't know. Somebody bring some blankets over here. Are you okay?"

"I guess so. I'm pregnant."

Garret wrapped a blanket around Tony while Ryan did the same with Christi.

"Let's get you back to civilization."

"Did you catch them?"

"We have a team working on that right now. They won't get away."

"But how will you find them?"

"The same way we found you." Garret pointed to the sky. "God bless our military."

XXVI

"Emily," Garret said. "Let me talk to Kelly."

"It's Wyatt."

Emily smiled and handed the phone to Kelly. Her hands trembled as she took it.

"Is he okay?"

"He's alive and healthy."

"Thank God. That sounds like there's a 'but' coming."

"He's been under a lot of strain. He hasn't said anything since we found him. Christi says that he was talking right up till then. I think he just needs some time to decompress. We're taking both of them to a hospital. I'll let you know where that is when we get there."

"Can't you give me an idea? I could get on my way."

"Broken Arrow. But don't come there. I doubt if they're equipped to handle this. They'll transfer him and Christi. I'll call from there and tell you where to go."

"Okay."

"Get Lois to watch the kids. Emily will drive you to the hospital."

"Okay. And thank you."

"Just doing my job."

***

The doctor turned to Garret. "He's in remarkable physical condition. His problems are beyond my field of expertise. I've given him a mild sedative. We should see in a short time if helping him relax brings him out of this state."

"And the girl?"

"Positive pregnancy test. I've ordered a complete blood work up on both of them. I'll arrange their transfer to Denver. However, they have no life threatening injuries. I see no reason to use an air ambulance."

"I want them transferred as quickly as possible."

"You're not a doctor. The use of an air ambulance is not justified."

"Fine. I'll get the helicopter. You make the other arrangements."

"Very well. If you insist on going that route."

"I insist." The doctor departed and Garret pulled aside the curtain to join Tony. "Hey, buddy, feeling any better?"

Tony looked up and sighed. "How will I ever face Kelly?"

"You didn't do anything wrong, Tony. You had to survive."

"No, I didn't have to survive. I just didn't want to die."

"There's nothing wrong with that."

"Survive, no matter what? I cheated on my wife to stay alive. I'm no better than an animal."

"Tony, you were raped."

Tony scowled for a few seconds, then turned his head away. "I'm tired."

Garret patted his shoulder. "You get some rest. You've earned it."

Concerned, Garret stayed with him until he fell asleep. Tony had taken what happened to him just as they had expected him to. He would need a lot of therapy to get over this. Or he might never recover. Garret clenched his fists. He hated to think that Tony would never be the same. And he felt that he had to accept some of the blame for that.

He strode across the emergency room to the cubicle that Christi occupied. She looked up from reading a magazine.

"How is he?"

Garret shrugged. "The doctor gave him something that made him relax enough to talk. But he's taking on an awful lot."

"Because of what he did with Sue?"

"Yeah."

"They would have killed him." She bit her lip. "He really considered it.

I saw it in his eyes. But I begged him not to leave me alone. I felt hopeless till I saw him. I was barely eating. He took care of me as much as he could. I told them that he was my half-brother so they'd let him close to me. When you catch Sue, she's pregnant."

He rubbed his hand over his face. "I suppose he knows."

"Yeah. He took it hard. He said he didn't want to think about it."

"What about you? How are you doing?"

"Couldn't be better. My life is so much better than it was forty-eight hours ago. I'm even excited about reading a three month old magazine. I'm kind of anxious to see Terri again. I used to hate school. Now I can't wait to get back. I'm going to have a baby. Life's good."

He gazed at her. "Where did you get this positive attitude?"

"I don't know. What I went through was just so awful. I became grateful for any little thing that made my life better. I'm so grateful for Tony. He probably saved my life. I would have gotten sick and died."

"He's pretty special."

"Tony's the greatest. I suppose they'll have a shrink talk to him. Maybe I can help. I want to do that."

"Good. It will probably help both of you."

***

Garret met Kelly at the main entrance of the Denver hospital. He hugged her before hugging his own wife.

"What can you tell me?" Kelly asked.

"Let's talk while we walk. It's quite a hike. They gave him a mild sedative in Broken Arrow. He relaxed enough to talk to me. In my uneducated opinion, his problem is guilt and shame. In his words, he cheated on you to stay alive."

"I was afraid of that. Maybe it will help when I tell him how much I love him."

"It can't hurt. They have a psychiatrist talking to him. Maybe he can tell us more."

When they reached Tony's room, a nurse told them that they would have to wait. Ten minutes later, a young doctor came from the room. The nurse pointed at Kelly and the doctor approached.

"Mrs. Wagner?"

"Yes. How is he?"

"I've given him a stronger sedative. I want to see how he responds after forty eight hours of rest. The stress and exhaustion are only exacerbating his symptoms."

"Can I see him?"

"He's nearly asleep. Go in now and I'll talk to you shortly."

When Kelly entered the room, she found Tony with his eyes closed. His full beard surprised her. Somehow, she had expected him to look exactly as he had the day he left. He opened his eyes when she said his name. She kissed his forehead.

"I love you, Tony."

"I love you. I'm so sorry."

"You came home. That's all that matters."

"No. I don't deserve you. I'm ...I'm a piece of trash."

"No, Tony. I love you. We need you. We needed you to come home. You would have let us down if you had let them kill you."

He turned his head away and closed his eyes. She stroked his hair until his breathing indicated that he had fallen asleep. She wiped her tears and left the room. When she found Garret talking on his cell phone, she remembered the sign ordering people to shut them off when they entered the building.

He nearly yelled. "How did you let that happen?" A pause while he listened. "Find him! You have access to the best technology out there. Don't mess this up!" He disconnected.

"They got away," Kelly said.

"Only one of them. The father covered the son and daughter's retreat. He kept my men pinned down till they neutralized him."

"He's dead?"

"Yeah. They caught the daughter, but the son slipped away."

"Son? I thought there were two sons."

"We found the other one buried in a cave. He'd been dead for a while."

"The one Tony wounded? He died from his wounds?"

"It was the one Tony wounded. But according to the Fisher girl, he recovered from that."

"Then how did he die?"

Garret sighed. "He pulled a knife on Tony and Tony killed him."

She caught her breath. "He's never killed anyone before." She bit her lip. "Why did they let him live after that?"

"Christi says the father considered that son a liability. He thought that Tony did him a favor. He started calling Tony his son after that."

She shuddered. "If he hadn't gotten them out when he did, he would have been completely brainwashed before long. Is that woman pregnant?"

"Christi thinks she is. We'll have her checked when we get her here."

"What will happen to the baby?"

"She'll be going to prison. Probably for life. The baby will be taken from her as soon as it's born."

"Then what?"

"That will be up to Tony. He'll have custody. How is he?"

"Asleep. But I talked to him for a minute. He called himself a piece of trash."

Emily hugged her. The psychiatrist came from another room and rejoined them.

"Mrs. Wagner, I would like to ask you some questions about your husband. Perhaps you would prefer a more private location."

"Maybe more comfortable. There is nothing I can tell you about Tony that I'd be afraid to have anyone hear."

"Nothing?"

"Tony almost finished the seminary." They followed him to a waiting room. "The only wild thing he's ever done in his life was one weekend with me before he entered the seminary. Even though he chose a different vocation, he still struggles to live his life as God would want him to. When the pastor goes on vacation, Tony preaches the sermon. You can't find anyone with a bad thing to say about him."

"I see. That at least partly explains the inordinate guilt he seems to be carrying. It will make my job more difficult."

Kelly thought about that for a moment. "Maybe you need to take a different approach."

"Such as?"

"I tried to tell him that what he did was okay, because it allowed him to come home to us. Maybe he needs to hear that it doesn't matter what he did, he's forgiven."

"But he's done nothing wrong. He doesn't need to be forgiven."

"In his mind, he has and he does."

"I cannot, in good conscience, take that approach."

Garret interrupted. "Aren't you supposed to tailor your treatment to meet the patient's needs?"

"To a certain extent."

"Kelly's right. I tried the same thing with Tony. We could fight for a long time to convince Tony that he's done nothing wrong. And we might eventually convince him. But we'd probably make a lot more progress, in his case, if we remind him that no matter what he's done wrong, he's forgiven. Once he remembers that, we can work on helping him see that having to choose between death and sex is no choice."

The psychiatrist removed his wire rimmed glasses and rubbed his eyes. "I cannot tell a person who has been raped that they need to be forgiven."

"Then get him a doctor who can." Garret's eyebrows nearly met. "Now."

"Mrs. Wagner?"

"I'm sorry. Yes. Someone who will use Tony's faith."

"I understand. We have another psychiatrist who may be a better fit."

"Thank you, doctor."

"Yeah, thanks, doc," Garret said. "Maybe you can answer a question for me. I've spoken to the Fisher girl. She seems to be fine. Why is Tony taking this so much harder?"

"She is not *fine*," the doctor replied. "Although she is remarkably resilient. I think what you're seeing is a basic difference in the way men and women are raised. In some cases women do accept blame when they are raped. Miss Fisher sees that she was forced by a bigger, stronger individual. Mr. Wagner is living with the stigma that a woman cannot force a man to engage in sexual intercourse. He is the bigger, stronger individual, therefore, he should always have the upper hand. He cannot see the threat of death as tipping the balance in her favor."

XXVII

Garret stared through the one way glass at Sue while he listened to the agent's report.

"She hasn't said much. She did say that Christi told her that her parents were alive when the brothers took the girls away. She doesn't know anything about murder. Claims that she's innocent. Tony came to them. Flirted with her right from the start. He wanted her. Says that she's carrying his baby."

"I want that confirmed with a test."

"It's been ordered."

"You read her her rights?"

"Of course. She hasn't requested a lawyer."

"A lawyer might say that she's too ignorant to ask for a lawyer. I don't know what I hope to accomplish by questioning her. She'll never give up her brother. We have all of them dead to rights."

"Do we? A good lawyer will say that she was just as much a victim as the Fisher girl. She was afraid of her father. He could even say that she wasn't responsible for kidnaping Tony. She claims that Tony enjoyed her company."

"The hell he did."

"But what will a jury believe if he can't testify?"

Garret glared long enough to make the agent fidget. "He'll be able to testify. And the Fisher girl will make a good corroborating witness."

"But the Brock woman could be very pregnant when this comes to trial. A good lawyer will try to make sure of that."

"Federal kidnaping and murder charges? That baby will be born long before she comes to trial. *We'll* make sure of that."

"So, what *do* you hope to accomplish?"

"Maybe I just need to face her. I'll see."

Garret opened the door and walked into the interrogation room. Sue looked up and gave a little smile.

"I never saw so many fine looking men at one time."

"Make you forget all about Tony."

"No. I could never forget Tony." She rubbed her belly. "He's the daddy of my baby. Me and Tony are in love."

"Tony is in love with his wife. Why do you think he took off the first time he had the chance?"

"Because he was worried about his sister. He never made a secret bout that."

"She's not his sister."

"Course she's his sister."

"They lied to you. They aren't related at all. They just knew you wouldn't let them near each other unless you thought they were related."

She scowled. "He still worried about her. You could tell it. Don't mean he don't love me."

"He loves his wife. He only bedded you because your father threatened to kill him if he didn't. You know what it's called when you threaten to kill someone if they don't have sex with you? Rape. You raped him."

"Can't rape a man."

"You're in for a surprise."

"Just let me talk to Tony. He'll straighten this out."

"You're not very bright. Tony wants nothing to do with you. He can't stand the sight of you. He doesn't love you."

She brushed tears away with an angry swipe. "You're a mean man. Tony loves his kids. He'll love my baby too."

"I want to be perfectly clear about something else. After that baby is born, you will never see it again. You are going to prison for life. Unless you help us catch your brother. Then we might be willing to make you a deal."

Now Sue had more tears than she could wipe away. "You'll take my baby away?"

"That's right. And you'll never have one that you can keep, unless you cooperate."

"Ain't right. Asking me to double-cross my brother."

"He left you behind."

"That's a lie. Pa told us to split up. Give us a better chance."

"You must have planned to meet somewhere."

"He just told us to get away." Garret shook his head and began to leave the room. She raised her voice. "I don't know where he is."

"Life in prison. No children. Ever. If your memory improves, let me know."

XXVIII

"Agent Garret?"

He turned in the hospital hallway, looking for the soft female voice. "Terri. How are you?"

"Better, since Christi's safe."

"Are you going up to see her?"

"Yeah."

"We can walk together. How is she?"

"She always was stronger than me. You remember what a wreck I was when you found me. She's just such a rock. And she's pregnant. Did you know she wants to keep the baby?"

"She told me. How do you feel about that?"

"I couldn't have done it. I was so grateful that I didn't get pregnant. I know most people won't understand why she would want to keep a baby that was made by a rapist. I didn't, until she explained it. This is Mom and Dad's first grandchild."

"I guess, if you look at it that way, it does change things."

"She can't quit talking about Tony. She says he's our big brother now. Sounded kind of strange at first. But with what he did for her, and me, it sounds like a nice idea. We always liked him anyway. Everybody does."

"Yeah. Christi told me that even Jacob liked him."

Terri shuddered. "That tells you something. Is he really dead?"

"Yes."

"And Seth?"

"Yes."

"Thank, God. I know that's not very Christian. But he was a sick, sick man. The first time he raped me, he said, 'You're not Sue, but you'll do.' When we got back to their camp, I found out that Sue was his sister. He always called me Sue when he raped me. He whispered it so Jacob wouldn't hear."

"You couldn't tell me this before."

"Lots of therapy. Christi thinks that we should live with Tony when everything settles down. What do you think of that?"

He just walked for a moment. "First I've heard of it. Guess you should bounce the idea off Kelly before you do anything else. Don't be too disappointed if she says no. I've stayed in their house. You wouldn't get your own room."

"That's not very important anymore. You saw how we lived. We had no privacy at all. I heard that Tony isn't doing so good."

"He's having a hard time. The doctor thinks rest will help. He was under a terrible strain, wanting to help Christi, but feeling helpless."

"I think that's how Christi felt about me. She told me that it was easier for her after she knew I was safe. And she was able to lean on Tony too."

"When Tony knew that she was safe, I guess he gave himself permission to fall apart."

"Maybe I shouldn't mention anything to his wife. She probably has enough on her mind."

Garret thought about it. "Well, give her a couple days. Then just mention the idea. I'll bring her to see you and Christi. We'll let Christi tell her how the idea came up. Just make sure that Christi understands that we don't want to put pressure on Kelly. Just plant the seed."

"Plant the seed. Okay."

"I'll see you in awhile."

He found Kelly by Tony's bedside.

"I see they got him a shave."

"They let me do it. They said I couldn't possibly wake him. He's lost a little weight."

"Yeah. He looks skinny. He didn't have any extra fat to lose."

"Do you think he'll be okay?"

"Eventually. But you need to be prepared for a long process."

"I think I am. His parents are coming tomorrow."

"Good. The doctor should wake him up by then. Come on. There are a couple of young ladies who would like to talk to you."

"Young ladies? Christi and Terri?"

"The same. I think they want to tell you what a hero your husband is."

"I already know that. Remember, I met him when he rescued me."

"I remember. Maybe you can tell them about that."

***

Tony opened his eyes and smiled at Kelly.

She kissed him. "I love you, Tony."

"I love you. I had the worst nightmare." He looked around the room and the smiled faded, replaced by a look of horror.

She reassured him. "I love you, Tony. You did what you had to. God forgives you."

"No-o."

He rolled over, turning his back to her. She rubbed his back, but he cringed.

"I love you. It doesn't matter what you did, Tony. I wanted you back. God forgives you."

He pulled away even farther, pressing himself against the bed rail. She removed her hands and he relaxed just a little.

Kelly sighed. He seemed no better after forty eight hours of rest. She sought out help at the nurses' station. "He doesn't even want me to touch him."

"I know." The nurse tapped a closed circuit monitor. "I've called Dr. Brown."

"I'll be with Tony."

When Dr. Brown and the nurse entered Tony's room, she gave him an injection. The psychiatrist, with deep crows feet and laugh lines, explained.

"It's a sedative, not strong enough to put him to sleep. Then we'll start him on anti-depressants. That will take several days to reach therapeutic levels. We'll do blood tests to monitor the level. Until then, we'll keep him mildly sedated. I'll be able to conduct sessions with him. But therapy will be more effective once he no longer needs the sedative."

"Whatever it takes to get my husband back."

Tony let go of the bed rail. After a while, he rolled over on his back and looked around.

"Mr. Wagner, how do you feel?"

Tony yawned. "Kind of groggy. Kelly." He bit his lip. "I'm sorry, Kelly. I cheated on you."

"I know, Tony. I forgive you. God forgives you."

"Mr. Wagner, everything you did, you did under duress. That makes whatever you did forgivable. Do you believe in forgiveness, Mr. Wagner?"

"Yes."

"Do you believe that you're forgiven?"

Tony glanced at Kelly. "Well, I suppose I am."

"That's right. You are. Think about that."

Tony frowned as if concentrating. Then he yawned again. Kelly kissed his forehead.

"God forgives you, Tony. I love you."

"I love you."

"Mrs. Wagner, why don't you take a break. I want to spend a little time with your husband."

Kelly nodded and left the room. Garret met her in the hall and gave her a quick hug.

"No better?"

"No. The doctor is putting him on anti-depressants."

"Well, I have some news that might help. The Brock woman isn't pregnant."

"Thank God. But everyone was so sure that she was?"

"She wanted it so bad that she convinced herself. The doctor says she's experiencing a false pregnancy. Her body is going through all the changes it would if she were really pregnant. She refused to believe the doctor when he told her that she wasn't."

"How long can she keep that up?"

"He said she would probably get over it in less than nine months. But that depends on how delusional she is. Come with me. Terri Fisher is in Christi's room. They'd like to talk to you."

"I'd like that. It helps a little to see the people he made this sacrifice for."

***

Kellyy found Christi and Terri sitting in the two chairs in Christi's room. When she saw Kelly, she bounded up and hugged her. Kelly hesitated before returning the gesture.

"Thank you," Christi said.

"For what?"

"For letting him do what he does. He saved my life. Both of our lives."

Kelly stepped back and wiped her eyes. "I ... I don't know if I can after this."

Christi squeezed her arm. "I understand. Have a chair. I'll sit on the bed. Any change?"

"The psychiatrist is with him now. He talked to Tony about forgiveness.

That seemed to get through to him."

Christi fingered the tie on her robe. "I feel so bad. I begged him to do it. I knew they'd kill him and I couldn't face life without him."

Kelly shook her head. "Christi, you saved *his* life. If you hadn't been there, he probably would have let them kill him. Thank *you*."

"You have to admire someone who's willing to die for what they believe."

Kelly pulled out a tissue and wiped her eyes. "I would have been so mad at him. I'm a little angry that he even considered it."

Both girls stared at her. Finally Christi nodded. "He would have been leaving you alone too."

"Yes. But that's the man I married. The man I love. Tony sees very few gray areas. He has a very strong sense of right and wrong."

"All we really knew about him before this is that he was a good guy. He kept doing things to remind people of that. I was so shocked when I saw him. But after I thought about it awhile, it made sense. I told them he was our half-brother."

"Garret mentioned that."

"I knew it was the only way they'd let me near him. I wasn't allowed to even talk to Seth and Terri couldn't talk to Caleb. But we lived with that lie for so long, I feel like he's my brother."

"I understand. What you've been through will bring two people close. Do you know the story of how Tony and I met?" Both girls nodded. "I couldn't forget him. I'm sure, when he's better, he'll tell me that he feels just as close to you."

"I hope so. I want to throw an idea out to you. Terri and I have discussed this. We're not asking anything more than that you think about it. Think about becoming our foster parents."

Kelly stared. *Three kids and a damaged husband, plus two teenaged girls. One of them pregnant! I can't do it.* She let her breath out.

"Thanks for giving me time to think about it. We'll have to see how Tony progresses."

"There's no rush at all. We can stay with the Petersons until you're ready."

XXIX

Kelly hugged Christi. "Bet you're glad to be getting out of here."

"Yeah. Just in time for school to start. The Petersons promised to take us shopping before we go home. Mrs. Peterson says there are some very fashionable maternity clothes. I'm sorry that I couldn't help Tony more."

"But you did help him. I don't think he blames himself so much anymore. After he gets better, I'll talk to him about having you two stay with us."

"That's cool. Until then, the Petersons are good foster parents and we've known them a long time. We'll get along fine."

"And you'll both keep seeing a counselor?"

"Twice a week for me, once for Terri. Guess she's not as messed up as I am."

"Hey, I was a lot more messed up," Terri said with a smile. "I saw someone every day for a month. They kept me in the hospital that whole time. You're going home after, what, ten days. I was way more messed up."

Kelly hugged them both, then watched them walk away.

She returned to Tony's room and found him sleeping. She wiped his mouth. Drooling seemed to be one of the side effects of the powerful anti-depressant the doctor had prescribed. She had asked for the warning label that came with the drug and was appalled by the long list of side effects. So far she had also noticed drowsiness, memory lapses, staggering, and evidently dry mouth. He seemed to be thirsty all of the time.

The doctor no longer had him on suicide watch. He had been moved to a different room. Nurses made sure that he dressed every morning and spent some of his time in the activity room of the psychiatric ward. Kelly found that experience depressing.

But it did not seem to bother Tony. He had trouble staying awake for more than an hour.

Dr. Brown reassured her that the intensity of these side effects would diminish as his body adjusted to the drug. And Tony did seem to be making progress in dealing with his experiences. But she wondered if the drug-induced progress would remain after the drugs were removed.

She walked to the window and stared out at the little courtyard where psychiatric patients could get some fresh air. She and Tony had walked there and sat together soaking up the late summer weather, but he barely seemed to notice. He never asked about the kids. He never initiated a conversation.

Kelly sighed, fighting her own depression. She faced the bed again. "Tony, I want you back."

He opened his eyes. "Hi."

"Hi. I miss you."

"Miss me?"

"You're not all here, Tony."

"Yeah. I noticed. Why?"

"It's the drugs they're giving you. They're helping. But they have side effects."

"They help, huh?"

"Yes. You were in pretty tough shape when you came in here."

"Oh. Couldn't they give me less?"

Kelly just blinked as he reached for his glass of water. "It would be worth a try. We'll ask Dr. Brown when he comes again."

***

To Kelly's surprise, Dr. Brown agreed without argument to decrease Tony's medication by one quarter. The difference took two days to show up in Tony's behavior. He stayed awake longer, drooled less, and staggered not at all. His mind worked better, yet his depression did not worsen.

Pastor Johnson stopped for another visit.

"Morning Pastor," Tony said, smiling.

"Well, that's a change for the better. I see life in your eyes again. Last time I wasn't sure if you recognized me."

"I probably didn't. Not so many drugs now. I plan to talk to the doctor today about cutting back some more and sending me home."

"That would be wonderful. Are you sure that you're ready for that?"

"I think so. I must be feeling better because I'm getting bored. But if I have to choose, I'll take less medication rather than going home. I understand that they want to see how I respond to a smaller dose."

"Where's Kelly?"

"I sent her home. She didn't want to go, but she really needed a break. Garret was headed to Spruce Lake anyhow. I finally got her to agree to it by asking her to bring the kids here on Saturday."

"They miss you. Especially Brett."

Tony sighed. "Justin probably doesn't even remember me."

"If he doesn't, it won't take him long. How are you, Tony?"

"A lot better."

"I'm sorry that I expected too much of you. I thought that you, of all people, wouldn't need to be reminded that all of your sins are forgiven."

"If it had happened once, I probably would have been okay. If I'd gotten out of there while it still made me sick to my stomach, I probably would have been okay. But I got used to it. For a while I had to make my brain think of something else. I think it was kind of like an out of body experience. But after awhile, it wasn't. I started enjoying it. It was the only way I could vent my anger and frustration. Or at least the most effective way. And that's what I had trouble forgiving myself for."

"Remember that you weren't just thinking of yourself. You had to protect Christi. And, in the end, because of the choices you made to survive, you brought her safely home."

"I did, didn't I. I hadn't even thought about that. But still, the end doesn't justify the means."

"No. But remember, 'all have sinned and come short of the glory of God.' My bad thought about my neighbor's loud music is every bit as condemning as murder. We all need forgiveness. You needed it just as much before this experience as you do now. And it's given freely to us all."

"Thanks, pastor. I think I'm really ready to go home and get back to my life."

***

"I hear they're talking about sending you home."

Tony grinned at Garret and set his Bible aside.

"Yeah. I'm down to half the anti-depressant they had me on to start with, and they may cut that back more before I leave. I feel like I wouldn't need it at all. I want to get home and spend time with the kids. And hopefully, before too long, I can get back to work."

"Don't rush things. Enjoy the time with your kids. You've missed too much."

"Yeah. When Kelly brought them to see me, I couldn't believe it. Justin remembered me. That made me cry."

"You're a softy."

"I have so many blessings. I forgot that for a while."

"You had a traumatic experience. That will mess with your head."

"I *guess* so."

Garret shifted in his chair. "Tony, there are some things I wanted to talk to you about while you're still here."

Tony waited for him to finish, then realized that he had. "In case they put me into a tailspin?"

"It may not be pleasant. I also need to get your statement."

Tony nodded. "Let's get it over with. Fire away."

"Do you know that we still haven't found Caleb?"

"Yeah. Doesn't surprise me."

"Do you have any suggestions?"

"I heard them talking about other camps, but the names they used didn't ring any bells. Split Pine and Bear Skull. They weren't along the river because their back door was in the cliff."

Garret made a note. "And they were headed away from the river when we caught up with them."

"Do you have a map?"

Garret pulled it from his pocket and they spread it on the bed. He pointed to a spot. "The team caught them here. Jacob took a stand, covering his kids' retreat. They split up. We caught Sue here." He indicated the point on the map. "By the time the helicopter pursued Caleb, he was gone."

"What happened to the UAV?"

"I insisted that it search for you. I got my butt chewed for that, but I'd do it again."

Tony studied the map for a moment, then circled an area with his finger. "You've probably already thought of this, but I'd search here."

"That's pretty close to Spruce Lake. You think he'd go back there?"

"They would have arranged to meet somewhere. When Jacob and Sue didn't show up, he knew that they were either captured or killed. Family means everything to these people. He can't help his father or Sue."

"Christi."

"And the baby she's carrying."

"Thank God the Petersons live right in Spruce Lake. I'll have someone watch the house anyhow. I'm not taking chances with those girls."

"Good. Is it really true that Sue isn't pregnant?"

"Yes. They even did an ultrasound. Nothing. False pregnancy."

Tony let his breath out. "That's the answer to a prayer."

"Will you be able to face her in court?"

A shudder shook Tony. "Yes."

"Do you believe that you were raped?"

"Yes. On a certain level. But part of me still says it's not possible. Won't it be kind of hard to get a conviction on that?"

"Yeah. The US Attorney didn't include rape on the indictment for Sue. Just kidnaping. How do you feel about that?"

Tony shrugged. "The kidnaping should be easy to prove. I can testify that she put a gun to my head and tied me up. It can't get any clearer than that. She should go away for a long time."

"She will. Even if she cuts a deal."

"Deal?"

"If she helps find Caleb."

"It'll never happen."

"That's what I figured. You say they would've had a place to meet. She says they just split up. So she's lying. You know, her attorney will probably still attack your credibility as a witness, because of the sex. Say you wanted to be there."

"Then I'll just show him these." He held out his wrists, still scarred from the handcuffs.

"Good. And we have pictures from when those wounds were fresh. We'll make sure the jury sees those too. Is there anything else you want to ask me about?"

Tony appeared to study the map a little longer. "You know that I killed

Seth?"

"Christi told us." When Tony said nothing else, he continued. "It was self-defense. They weren't letting you carry a knife. He attacked you, and you took it from him."

"But I planned it."

"You what?"

"I could see how much he hated me. He couldn't have Sue as long as I was there. So, I provoked him. I rubbed salt in the wound to make him mad enough to attack me. And it worked. He fell right into my trap. It was premeditated."

"You knew he would try to kill you and you wanted to get it over with?"

"Yes. I was afraid he'd get the chance to do it when my hands were cuffed. He wouldn't have cared about a fair fight. He wanted me dead."

"Tony, that's just premeditated self-defense. If you'd waited behind a rock and brained him with a club, then we could discuss premeditation. And you'd still probably get off with justifiable homicide. You just planned it to give him the least advantage. Do you believe that?"

Tony nodded. "I always did. I guess I just needed to hear you say it."

"No doubt about it. Okay. That's everything I wanted to tell you." Garret pulled out a recorder. "Let's get started on your statement."

XXX

A week later, Tony climbed into Garret's car in front of the hospital. His medication had been reduced to one fourth the original dose. He would see a counselor twice a week, but no return to work had been scheduled. That would depend on how he adjusted to his old life.

"Want anything to eat before we start back?"

"Kelly has my favorite supper planned. But I'd love a milk shake. An extra large one."

Garret chuckled. "Good as done."

He pulled into the drive-thru of a fast food restaurant, bought Tony a chocolate shake and himself coffee before heading out of Denver.

When Tony finished his shake, he heaved a contented sigh. "It will be good to be home."

"Amen."

"You were away from home almost as long."

"Not quite the same. And Emily moved down there with me more than a month ago. Figured it was the only way to see me."

"Be careful. When people spend any time in Spruce Lake, they never want to leave."

"You're not the first person to tell us that. Have you and Kelly discussed the Fisher girls?"

"Yeah. What do you think of that idea?"

"It would be a serious change for you and Kelly. You'd suddenly have two moody teenaged girls, one of them pregnant. And I have a feeling it would be harder for Kelly than for you."

"I think you're right. I'm having trouble seeing any downside to taking them in."

"How many bathrooms in your house?"

"Oh. One."

"One and a half. Did you forget that you were scheduled to move this summer?"

"Oh. Then that shouldn't be a problem."

"Teenaged girls can take hours in the bathroom."

"That's right. I have sisters. I should have thought of that."

"And in six months or less, one of those girls will have a baby."

"I know. Do you think Kelly really hates this idea?"

"What did she say?"

"Let's just think about this for a while."

"No. I don't think she hates the idea. I think she has a healthy scepticism."

"Maybe I should just let her make the decision."

"Talk to her about it. And don't rush into it. Both of you need some time to get your lives back on track."

***

Tony spent all afternoon with his children, almost always holding or hugging one of them. He and Kelly contented themselves with brief hugs and kisses. They let Brett and Christina stay up well past their bedtimes, making up for lost time. Tony carried his daughter to bed after she fell asleep, then guided Brett to his room.

He smiled. "This is a nice house."

"A lot more room." Kelly took his hand. "Let's go to bed."

"Okay." But he just shuffled after her.

"I know this might be tough for you. No pressure." She closed the bedroom door and began unbuttoning his shirt. "Let me know if anything I do feels uncomfortable."

"You've never done it very often, but don't lick me. Okay?"

"Okay. Not anywhere?"

"Not for now."

"I'll do my best."

"I'm really not very interested. I should be."

She caressed his lips. "That could be the medication. It's one of the side effects."

"It is? I'm glad you told me. I thought I felt this way because of what I did."

"What you did brought you back to me."

"The doctors ran all kinds of tests. I didn't catch anything that I could give to you."

"I know. Now, let's just be quiet and let me show you how much I love you."

He just smiled. With tender motions, she undressed him. They kissed for a very long time before he removed her clothes. Then they just hugged. Tony sighed several times before he inhaled the scent of her hair. Kelly did not interrupt him, letting him decide when he was ready to go on.

He looked into her eyes. "I've never felt so loved. But maybe it's never been this important to me."

"And maybe I've never loved you quite so much. They say you never really appreciate what you have till it's gone."

"You appreciated me."

"Not as much as I do now."

He wiped her tears and grinned. "I love you. We've done enough crying for a while. Tonight's about happiness. Let's see how much happiness we can stand."

She laughed and they kissed again. He carried her to the bed, as strong as he had ever been. Passionate foreplay took longer than usual to arouse him.

But before they could finish what they started, his body lost interest.

She caressed his cheek. "That's okay. We'll just try again."

"Trying is a lot of fun too."

She chuckled and resumed her efforts. Twice more, he could not maintain his interest long enough to finish. He flopped back on the bed.

"You're sure it's the drugs?"

She kissed his chest. "Almost positive."

"Can't say that I much care for the side effects."

"Me either. The other side effects have gone away since they lowered the dose."

"What other side effects?"

"Drooling. Staggering. Sleepiness. Short attention span."

"Wow." He thought a moment. "Now I just have S-A-D-D."

"Sadd?"

"Sexual Attention Deficit Disorder."

They both laughed, then she hugged him.

"Glad you can joke about it."

"I can now, because I'm just enjoying being with you so much. But I can see how this could get frustrating real fast." He sighed. "I want to quit taking the medication."

Kelly squeezed him. "I think you're ready to get along without it. But ask the doctor first. I don't want you thinking about killing yourself."

"I wouldn't. I never thought about that."

"Never?"

"No. Really. Although it got so bad that I wished they would kill me. And when I thought about them catching me again, I hoped that they would kill me. I might have even done something to make that happen."

"That would have been suicide."

"Yeah. I guess so. But that's just because I felt so hopeless. I don't have any reason to feel hopeless now."

"No. But I've studied depression lately. Hopelessness can just be a symptom. Depression can be the reason."

"Okay. I'll talk to the doctor before I quit taking the medication. And after I quit, I'll be talking to the counselor twice a week. She can keep an eye out for symptoms."

"Good enough."

***

The next morning Tony called Dr. Brown, who advised against discontinuing the medication. After Tony explained his motivation, he suggested a different anti-depressant with a low risk of sexual side effects.

"I appreciate that, doctor. But I'd like to try to go without first. I think I've recovered enough to do that. Between my faith and the counselor, I think I'll be okay."

"Very well. But would you at least do it this way. Cut the pill in half. Take that for ten days. You should see an improvement in your sexual performance within a few days. Toward the end of that ten days, pay special attention to your mood. I'll speak to your counselor and have her do the same. If at the end of that time it seems advisable, you may discontinue the medication. With careful monitoring of your condition."

"Sounds fair."

"Do not even consider discontinuing your counseling sessions."

"Why would I do that?"

"Poor judgement. Depression. At this point, any number of reasons. None of them good."

"I agree. I know I can't just snap back from what I've been through. I haven't even left the yard since I got home. Don't worry. I'll do that today.

I have a lot of things to deal with and I'm sure I'll need some help with it."

"That's an excellent attitude. Remember, it could be something very small that triggers a reaction. It does not have to be the sight of handcuffs or a gun. It could be the handcuff keys or a bullet."

"I'll try to keep that in mind."

XXXI

Later that day the entire family walked to park headquarters. Don greeted Tony with a vigorous hand shake that lingered.

Tony smiled. "I'm glad to see you too, Don."

"You going to quit working for the FBI now?"

"Hey. If you'll recall, I was shot while working for the park service. If you think I shouldn't have a dangerous job, I should have been a minister."

Don growled. "Never mind. I'll just be happy when you come back to work."

"I'm sorry I left you shorthanded this summer."

"And how was that your fault?"

"I guess because I was working for the FBI."

Don waved a hand of dismissal. "I blame Garret. And, besides, the park service sent me a seasonal worker to take your place. You came back just in time."

"I feel like I could come back to work Monday. But the doctor says I should wait awhile."

"Don't worry about it. The busy season is over. Take the time you need."

"Maybe in a week, they'll at least let me work in the office. They might want me to wait a while before I carry a gun."

"We can work with that."

They visited for a little longer, then the family walked to the stable to see Chance. Tony saddled him and took the kids for rides around the park buildings. Kelly snapped pictures, especially of Tony and Justin.

"His first ride."

Tony grinned. "I'm glad that I'm here for it."

"Me too."

He unsaddled and groomed Chance, letting Brett and Christina help him. Then they returned to the house. He kissed Kelly.

"How would you feel about having Christi and Terri over for dinner on Sunday?"

"I think I'll be ready to share you by then. Did you want to invite the Petersons too?"

"Ah-h. No. I'll call them and explain. If we're thinking about becoming their guardians, we need to get a feel for what that would be like. I hope they understand."

"I think they will. Christi and Terri have told them about the idea."

His brow furrowed. "Do you think Terri really wants it?"

"I'm not so sure about that. I think she may just be going along because Christi wants it. Because of loyalty, or maybe guilt."

"Survivor guilt?"

"The shoe would probably fit. She had to leave Christi behind and Christi ended up pregnant while she didn't."

"Makes sense."

"You haven't really said how you feel about taking in two teenaged girls, one of them pregnant."

He gave her a crooked smile. "Haven't I?"

"No. Although it seems like you want to."

"I think I do. If it were just Christi, I'd say yes. We lived with that lie for so long that I started to think of her as my sister. We're that close. I want to feel that way about Terri. But I don't know if we can develop that kind of relationship. We just haven't been through the things Christi and I went through."

"You will never be that close to Terri. Christi trusts you with her life."

"You haven't said how you feel about this."

"I'm cautious." She smiled. "And not for the reason you might think. Christi is a beautiful seventeen-year-old girl. You're her knight in shining armor."

Tony stared, then grinned. "You've got to be kidding."

"No. You rescued me and I fell for you."

"I'm the same age as you are and I wasn't married at the time. She thinks of me as her big brother."

"I hope so."

"Okay. It's something to consider and I'll keep it in mind."

***

On Sunday, Christi and Terri walked home with them after church. Tony held Kelly's hand while Christi clung to his other arm. Christina offered to hold Terri's hand and she accepted. Brett pushed Justin in his stroller. Everyone talked about school.

When they reached the house, Christi insisted on helping Kelly set the table. Terri pitched in with a little less enthusiasm. The national park and community provided material for dinner conversation. After everyone helped clear the table, they watched from the deck while Brett and Christina played in the back yard.

Christi hugged Tony and he wrapped his arm around her shoulders. He noticed Terri give them a dirty look.

"Kelly, will you excuse us? We need to have a little talk."

"Sure." She kissed him.

"Come on, Terri. Just the three of us." He kept his arm around Christi and Terri skulked along. When they reached the livingroom, he chose a chair and the girls sat on the sofa. "Before we can think seriously about having you two move in here, we need to have an honest discussion. Terri, I don't want to feel like we're shoving this down your throat. I want to know what you think of the idea."

"I want whatever Christi wants."

"Nobody wants exactly what someone else wants. Don't be a 'yes man'. Tell us how you feel."

She glared at him. "I don't know if it's such a good idea."

"That's better. Why?"

She glanced at Christi, then nearly spat her next words. "She has a crush on you."

Christi's face turned scarlet. "I do not! Why would you say that?"

"You're always talking about him. And the first chance you get, you're hanging all over him. You do the math."

"Okay." Tony nodded. "I can see how you could get that impression. Christi, you obviously disagree. Tell us."

"I don't have a crush on you. But I guess I can see how Terri got that impression too. I do talk about you all the time. But I think of you as my big brother. Ah-h." She covered her face with one hand, then lowered it. "Although I guess I mentioned that you have a really great body."

This time Tony blushed. "Not exactly the kind of thing you're supposed to notice about your brother."

"Well, it was tough not to. But it doesn't mean that I have a crush on you. And Terri, didn't you notice that I've been 'hanging all over you' since I came back?"

Terri pursed her lips. "You almost never hugged me before. Now you can't seem to get enough."

"I can't get enough of the people I love. I did the same when grandma was here. I love Tony almost as much as I love you. If he hadn't been there, I probably would have starved myself to death. I owe him my life. I need him to be part of our family. Do you understand?"

Terri looked from Christi to Tony, then wiped a tear away. "Tony, you helped save my life too. Christi got me loose and you got me out of that canyon. You covered my escape and they caught you. You went through those three months for us."

He shrugged. "I was just trying to do the right thing. The Lord put us in the right place at the right time to help you. He never gives us more than we can handle. I guess He knew that I could handle more than you could."

"He was right. I was falling apart. Christi didn't eat much. I didn't eat at all. Now I think I understand how she feels about you. If you'll have us, I'd really like to live with you."

"Kelly and I need to talk it over some more. And I think that Brett should have a say too. And I suppose we should run this by the counselor."

"I already have," Christi said. "She kind of hinted that I shouldn't get my hopes up. Are you seeing the same counselor as we do?"

"Yeah. I guess she's the only one who comes to Spruce Lake. Come on. It's too nice a day to spend inside. You know that I'll be a strict guardian, don't you."

They stood and he wrapped an arm around each of their shoulders.

"What else could we expect from the Reverend?" Terri said.

Christi laughed. "Besides, it's not like I'm going to go out and get myself pregnant."

They were all laughing when they returned to the porch.

Kelly smiled. "Looks like we'll be increasing the size of our family."

"If we can get the approval of the rest of the family," Tony said. "And our mental health professionals."

XXXII

Tony left Justin in Lois's care before he accompanied Brett and Christina to school. Then he circled the town, about a two mile walk, enjoying the fresh air, but feeling vulnerable.

He could not maintain his normal pace because of the number of people who stopped him to shake his hand or hug him. Everyone in town knew what he had done to survive. And they all supported the decisions that had brought him home. Three times his elderly lady friends brought him to tears with their heartfelt greetings.

At ten o'clock, he arrived at the clinic for his appointment with the counselor. After an intense, productive session, he felt drained. He continued walking, hoping the fresh air would perk him up. He found his way to the sheriff's office.

Ryan shook his hand much like Don had. He led the way to the conference room where Garret and another FBI agent studied files.

Garret grinned. "Good to see you out and about."

"Feels strange to be able to go wherever I want to."

"Is it working? Can you go anywhere?"

"So far. I had to push myself a little to go down tenth street with those thick trees along both sides. But I made it through."

"Good. Graham, go ahead and make those calls." The other agent left while Tony and Ryan settled into chairs. "How's family life?"

"Making up for lost time."

"I hear you had the Fisher girls over for dinner yesterday," Ryan said.

"Yeah. I think they'll be moving in with us after we've had a little time to enjoy being a family again. We're talking with the counselor about it."

"How soon?" Garret asked.

"At least a month."

"Okay. Let me know when the time comes. We'll have to consolidate our stakeouts."

Tony nodded, then frowned. "Stakeouts?"

"I don't want to take chances with you either."

"I appreciate that."

"We heard that you've started martial arts lessons."

"Yeah. I never did anything beyond what was required in peace officer training. When they had me, I felt pretty helpless without my gun. I want to change that."

"Seems like a good idea to me. What's your counselor think?"

"She really grilled me before she agreed. Anything new?"

"We've been searching the area you suggested. The UAV isn't much use because there are quite a few hikers around."

"A foot search?"

"We're out on horseback, searching caves and isolated areas. But we have two choppers up with infrared equipment. When they find human heat signatures, they can do a visual check. We found evidence that someone had camped in a cave about fifteen miles from here. Could be anyone, but we've sent hair to the lab for DNA analysis."

"Fifteen miles?"

"Yeah. How do you feel about that?"

"Uneasy. And that's overreacting a little. Like you say. Could be anyone."

"You have the right to overreact. But everyone is on the alert. Caleb's pictures are plastered all over the area. We're watching out for him."

"Anyone would recognize him, unless he alters his appearance."

Garret scowled. "I'd hoped you wouldn't think of that."

"I don't have 'stupid' written on my forehead. And neither does Caleb.

If he wants to get Christi back, he'll shave, cut his hair, and steal regular clothes."

"We've told people to report if anything goes missing, not just valuables. We want to hear from them if they just think they've misplaced something."

"We get a call or two every day," Ryan said. "We check them all out."

"Anything promising?" Tony asked.

"Maybe. Out near that cave. Some food and an old pair of shoes."

"What size?"

"Size? I'll check and see if we got that information."

Ryan left the room and Tony raised his palms.

"Caleb had bigger feet than I do. Probably a twelve."

Garret smiled and shook his head. "I forgot about your powers of observation for a little while there. And I thought you might not consider that he'd altered his appearance."

"There's something else you should know. Caleb probably has my Kevlar vest."

"Yeah. I'd say that's something we should know. If we need to take him down, we'll have to go for a head shot. While we're on the subject. When I took Terri and left you to cover us, I distinctly remember telling you to shoot to kill. But you didn't do that."

Tony ran his hand through his hair. "Well, I considered your advice ..."

"Advice? That was an order."

"Oh. Sorry. I misunderstood."

"I'll bet you did."

"I'm a lousy shot?"

"Keep digging. You're just about deep enough to bury yourself."

"I asked myself which would slow them down more. Having a man killed? Or having a man with a leg wound? It made a lot of sense at the time.

I didn't realize how carefully they'd planned their escape."

"Uh-huh."

"And hind sight's twenty-twenty. If I'd killed Seth then, I wouldn't have had to kill him later. Guess you were right."

"I guess so. But you were right too. If they hadn't had somebody covering their escape, it would have slowed them down enough for us to catch up to them."

Ryan's absence lingered. When he finally returned, he apologized. "Sorry. We didn't have that information. I had to call out there. The shoes were a size twelve and a half."

Garret walked to a wall map and used a red marker to circle a small black x. He moved on to a bulletin board and pulled out a pin holding a stack of notes. He removed one from the sheaf and pinned it at the top of the bulletin board, before returning the others to their place.

"Significant. We'll get a sketch artist to work up a drawing of him without the beard."

"How accurate will that be? Nobody except Sue has seen him without a beard since he was a kid."

"We have a school picture when he was about twelve. The artist can use one of those computer programs to age it. That will be good enough for people to keep an eye out for him."

"What should I do?"

"Just lock your doors at night and stay out of the woods for now."

"Okay, for now."

***

Kelly noticed the look in Tony's eyes during supper. This night, they hurried the kids off to bed. They stood in the kitchen, kissing for a very long time before he carried her to the bedroom. They accomplished stripping at a much quicker pace than the first time. His body responded to far less stimulation.

Yet when he laid her on the bed, he still lost interest. He sighed and rolled over on his back. Kelly kissed his chest.

"It was better that time. Is it still the medication?"

"I don't think so. I just ... had a thought."

"About what?"

"The things I did."

"Guilt?"

"Yeah."

"Whatever you did, you did it so you could come home to us. I would have been really mad at you if you had let them kill you when you could have prevented it."

He gazed at her. "Really?"

"Really. I need you. We need you. I think I told Garret that I wanted you to come home no matter how many commandments you had to break."

"I broke several."

"And you're forgiven. Please forgive yourself. Let it go."

He gave her a soft kiss. "I'll work on it. Now, let's try this again."

This time, he finished what he started. But as he caught his breath, his mind flashed back to Sue. He shook his head to fight off the image.

"Are you okay?"

"Yeah. Just a little flashback. I'll be fine."

She caressed his cheek. "Do we need to talk about it?"

He forced a smile. "Do you need to talk about it?"

"I'm so angry about what they did. All of them."

He nodded. "I've been able to lay the blame on Jacob. I think Caleb and Sue would have become pretty normal people if they'd been raised like normal people. Seth was just sick. I think he would have gotten into trouble either way."

"He tried to kill you."

"Yeah. It was a fatal mistake."

She studied him. "You're not second-guessing yourself about that at all."

"If I hadn't killed him, he would have come after me again. I wish he hadn't forced me to do that. Even after I chose law enforcement, I never thought I'd have to kill anybody. But I can't change the past."

"I'm glad you killed him. It brought you home to us."

He kissed her. "Is there anything else you need to talk about?"

"When you were with her ..." She bit her lip. "You said that you started to enjoy it."

"And you want to know how I could?"

"No. I can see how it was your only release for the anger and frustration you must have felt. It's more like ... Did you do the same things we do?"

He smoothed her hair. "No. In the beginning, when I was trying to buy time till Garret could find me, I used all my foreplay techniques to keep her entertained." He let his breath out. "It was a real low point when he went past on the river."

"I'm sorry. I shouldn't have asked you to talk about this."

"Yes, you should. "When I realized that I had to have sex with her, I channeled my anger. But that wasn't enough. I just mentally left my body. Let it respond to her. She was real aggressive. I thought of it as autopilot."

She caressed his cheek, letting him continue without prompting.

"After awhile, I'd use foreplay to bribe her. I knew the river would be my best escape route. I needed to scout downstream and along the bank. So I'd promise her something she really liked if we could go to a certain spot. Otherwise, sex was pretty one-sided. She did all the work and I finished the act."

"Thank you for telling me."

"Thank you for making love to me. Making love is so much better than sex."

"It was my pleasure. I've missed so many things about you. But I've really missed that."

He smoothed her hair. "I love you so much. I don't ever want to be away from you for that long again."

"I don't even want to be away from you overnight for a long time. I love you."

"Amen. If the FBI calls, I'll tell them I'm not available for a while. By the way, I believe I promised you a weekend just to ourselves, way back last spring."

"Yes, you did. Right now, having you home is enough. And the kids need this time with you too."

He nodded. "But we need that weekend. Before we have Christi and Terri move in, we need to take that weekend."

"Okay. But let's not go as far as Denver. How about the Elk Horn Bed & Breakfast?"

"Sounds nice. I'll see if they have an opening toward the end of the month."

Kelly kissed his neck. "It will be wonderful having you to myself for a whole weekend."

XXXIII

After their Friday meeting, Tony's counselor approved his return to limited duty.   Tuesday through Thursday, working only around park headquarters and not carrying a gun. After the first three days, she would evaluate how he had handled the experience.

He nearly ran to headquarters with the news.   Don took his announcement with his usual gruff demeanor. "Well, it's better than nothing."

Tony grinned. "Oh, admit it. You'll be glad to have me back."

"I *have* missed ribbing you, reverend. But I'll try to be a little more sensitive after what you've been through."

"That wouldn't be you, Don."

"No. Guess it wouldn't."

Tony left headquarters and walked around to the front of his house, intending to pull weeds in the flower beds. An unfamiliar car parked on the street grabbed his attention. A woman sat behind the wheel. He eased his way toward the front steps, keeping his eyes on her.

When she climbed from the car, he knew that he had never met her. Yet she looked so familiar that his heart began to pound. He climbed the steps sideways to keep her in sight.

"Mr. Wagner."

He grabbed the doorknob. *Locked! My God! I have to get away!* His eyes darted left and right, but his feet refused to move.

Through his panic, he noticed her hands fly to her mouth and tears come. *Why am I so scared? It's just a woman. And not a very big one.* He forced himself to take slow, deep breaths and try to think. *Her accent. I know that accent.* Panic threatened to overtake him again. *Sue looks just like her.*

She spoke. "I'm so sorry. I shouldn't of come. But, I have my answer." She started to get into her car.

"Wait."

She just stood beside the car as more than a minute passed. Tony's breathing returned to normal. He fumbled in his pocket for the house key. He showed her a palm, then with shaking hands, unlocked the door and pushed it open.

He turned back to her. "Now I have an escape route."

She nodded. "I'm so sorry. I needed to come see you to prove to myself that my daughter is delusional."

"Does she still believe that I love her?"

"Yes. She's convinced that you'll come to her rescue. She keeps saying that you'll straighten everything out. That you just left to protect the girl."

"She doesn't get that I did everything to protect the girl. I couldn't do that if I let Jacob kill me. I had sex with Sue to stay alive."

"I'm so sorry. It's my fault. When Jacob took the boys, I should of gotten as far away as possible. But I-I always hoped they'd get tired of living like that and come home."

He descended the steps. "I understand wanting to see your kids again."

"I'll try to talk Sue into pleading guilty. Tell the FBI everything she knows. It's the only way she's ever getting out of prison."

"Do you think you can convince her?"

"First I have to change her mind about you."

"I might be able to help with that. I think I need to confront her. I'll talk to Agent Garret."

"Can I come round the car?" He nodded and she just covered that distance, leaning on the hood. "Maybe having you tell her will do it. Thanks for offering. Can I ask you something?"

"I can't stop you."

"You killed Seth. He had it coming?"

He clenched his jaw before answering. "Yes. And I don't regret it."

"I understand." She wiped tears away. "Sue told me about it. The boy was never quite right. Never took the blame for his problems. Thought everything would of been fine if somebody or something had been different. If he got caught in a lie, it was Caleb's fault for telling on him. That sort of thing. I worried about how he'd turn out long before Jacob took him."

"He would've gotten in trouble no matter what. I think Caleb and Sue would have turned out okay if Jacob hadn't brainwashed them."

"I should of gone back to Arkansas when he left me. But he said he'd come see them. I just couldn't take them away from their pa."

Tony took another step toward her. But he had no trouble resisting his natural urge to hug a woman in distress. "You did the best you could under the circumstances."

"Thank you." She wiped her eyes again. "I'll leave you be now. You tell that FBI agent that I'll help get Sue talking if it can knock some time off her sentence."

"I'll do that." He watched her walk around the car. "I'm glad you came."

"How's that?"

"This helped me."

"It's good to undo some of the damage my family's done."

***

Garret welcomed even a hint of a break. He agreed to talk to the US Attorney in charge of the case, who would arrange a meeting with Mrs. Brock and Sue's lawyer.

Tony let go of the outcome. He had more important things to think about.

On Tuesday, he beat both Kelly and Don to work. A backlog of paperwork took up most of his first morning. When he found his mind wandering, he volunteered to go to the stable to clean stalls. After lunch, he took another stab at paperwork. But again, he felt distracted within an hour. He returned to the stable, swept the aisles and cleaned saddles, before tackling the paperwork a third time.

He reported to Don. "I got over half of it done, but I seem to have a short attention span. If I take a break—do something physical—I can get back to it."

"Whatever works. Just get it done this week. Somebody needs to do the grunt work too. And I don't think anybody will complain because they don't get to clean stalls or stack firewood."

"Probably not."

Tony stuck to that pattern during his other two days, feeling like a productive member of society again.

On Friday, he mentioned it to his counselor. "But I'm a little concerned about my attention span. I only remember having this problem a few times. And I always knew how to cure it."

"How was that?"

He blushed. "Getting some quality time with my wife."

"That isn't the problem now?"

"No."

"Your attention span will probably improve with time. Stay aware of the problem. We'll discuss it. Continue your three-day work week until I think you're ready for more."

***

On Friday evening, Tony and Kelly took their family for supper at the Peterson's. Floyd and Marsha had raised six kids before taking in a long list of foster children. In addition to Christi and Terri, they currently provided a loving home for three boys, ages six through ten.

Tony and Floyd watched the younger children playing in the back yard before supper. Tony tried to listen to Floyd, but found himself increasingly distracted. As distraction turned to anxiety, his eyes darted to the thick trees behind the house.

"Tony, are you alright?"

"What?"

"You look kind of pale."

"Something doesn't feel right."

Floyd frowned. "Do you think there's danger?"

"I don't know."

"Boys! Brett. Christina. Come in. It's time to wash up for supper." He lowered his voice. "Should I call the FBI agents?"

"I don't know."

"Let's run this by Kelly."

"You're a little early," Marsha said. "Oh, Tony, you're white as a sheet."

"Something made him nervous. I wondered if we should call the FBI agents."

Kelly held Tony's hands. "Did you see something?"

"No. I don't think so. I just started getting anxious. It's better now that I'm inside."

"Do you think we should call Garret?"

"No. I think it was some kind of anxiety attack. I just don't know what triggered it."

"I bet I do," Christi said, gaining everyone's attention.

"What?"

She held out her hand. "Come with me."

Tony looked at Kelly, then took Christi's hand. She led him back to the deck while the others followed. As Christi approached the hot tub, Tony began dragging his feet. His eyes grew wider and she met more resistance. He finally pulled away and fled back to the house, gasping.

When his breathing returned to normal, he stared at Christi. "The hot tub?"

"The first time I climbed into it, I dealt with some very bad memories. And he hardly ever took me to the hot spring. She took you there twice a day some days."

He nodded. "But it seems pretty silly to panic over a hot tub."

Kelly hugged him. "The things that trigger your fears aren't silly. Just something else to talk to your counselor about."

"Yeah." He let his breath out, then chuckled. "I'm sure glad we didn't call the FBI."

XXXIV

As he walked up the steps to the sheriff's office, Tony had to admit that he felt nervous. When he had confessed what he had done to his counselor, she had assured him that his actions had been appropriate. But he still had his doubts.

She had told him to share the information with Garret. But the closer he came to that eventuality, the more ashamed he felt. All the progress he had made since coming home seemed to be evaporating.

He hesitated at the door. One of the deputies left the building, startling him.

"Hi, Tony."

"Hi. Is Garret in?"

"Yeah."

Tony entered and asked the dispatcher the same question. She rolled her chair back and leaned over to get a better view of the conference room door.

"Yeah. But the door's closed. They must be doing something real important. They hardly ever close the door."

"Okay. Ryan doesn't look too busy. I'll bother him for a while."

But just as he entered Ryan's office, his phone rang. Ryan waved him to a chair, then Tony waited, fidgeting until he finished his call. Ryan disconnected and studied him a moment.

"You look like a kid who's been called to the principal's office. What's wrong?"

"I just need to talk to Garret about something."

"You look like you expect him to jump you about it." Tony shrugged. "Okay. You don't want to talk about it. I'll call back there. See if he's done with whatever was so all fired important that he needed to close the door."

He made the call, said only what he needed to, and waved Tony back.

Tony walked to the conference room, and opened and closed the door behind him.

"You can leave that open."

"I'd rather not."

"Something wrong?"

Tony shifted from one foot to the other. "I need to tell you something."

"Well, sit down and tell me."

Tony sat on the edge of a chair, stared at the floor, and sighed. "I did something. And I'm pretty ashamed of it."

"Something I don't know about?"

"Yeah."

"So tell me about it. How bad can it be?"

"Bad."

"The easiest way is to just spit it out."

Tony sighed again, then the words came fast. "For quite a while before I escaped, they didn't even worry about me getting my hands on their guns. I could have gotten one almost any time. Except at night. They always kept me handcuffed at night."

He took a breath and Garret made a point. "But you had Christi to think about."

"Yeah."

"And did a gun fit into your escape plan?"

"No. I mean, it would have been handy to have one along. But the way I had it planned, we needed a head start. I couldn't have had that if I'd pulled a gun on them."

"So what's the problem?"

"I'm not done."

"Sorry. Go on."

"I did get a gun in my hands, not long before we escaped. Caleb handed it to me so I could keep watch while he cleaned a deer."

"Hm-m. Isn't that something. You'd really gained their trust."

"But I should have used it. I should have shot him. Or at least clubbed him with it and tied him up. I just stood there and kept watch. And shot a bear."

"A bear. I can't imagine you shooting someone who wasn't shooting at you. Did you have a rope?"

"Yeah. We used it to drag the deer back home."

"Okay. So let's say you knocked out Caleb and tied him up. What would have been your next move?"

Tony blinked. "I guess I would have gone back to the cave. And waited. For someone to start missing us. Hopefully, that would have been Jacob."

"So you would have what? Shot him when he came out?"

Tony scowled at the problem, thinking about the area around the cave. "I would have just about had to."

"So that leaves Sue in the cave with Christi. Seth was already dead, right?"

"Yeah."

"But Sue hears the shot. Do you think she'd come rushing out to see what happened?"

"No. No way."

"So you still have Sue in the cave with Christi. And she's just as dangerous as the other two. She'd have used Christi as a human shield. And you'd have surrendered rather than let Christi get hurt."

"Yeah. I suppose."

"Then you would have had them ticked off at you. You would have lost their trust and blown any chance you had to escape."

"You make it sound like I made the right decision."

"You did! I know how your mind works, Tony. You don't like surprises. You're a very methodical guy. You plan things. You have backup plans. You consider every angle. That's what makes you a good detective. And it's why the escape plan you came up with worked."

Tony covered his face with his hands and rested his elbows on his knees. He did not cry, but let the relief wash over him. Garret watched him a moment, then began needlessly rearranging papers on the table. Finally, Tony sat up, the tension gone from his face.

"I was so ashamed of that, I didn't even remember it till last week. Kelly noticed that something was bothering me and told me that I needed to talk to my counselor about it. But even she had to pry it out of me. When she insisted that I had to tell you about it, I wanted to die. It was one thing to admit it to her and have her tell me I did the right thing. I was scared to death to tell you."

"Now see how much better you feel."

"A lot better. Thanks."

"Tony, anything you did while you were a captive was done under duress. No one can hold you up to the usual standards under those conditions. No one, including you."

"Okay."

"So if anything else comes up that you feel really ashamed of, remember that. And don't be afraid to talk to your counselor about it."

"Okay."

"But shooting a bear out of season. I'm not sure if the game warden would agree with me."

Tony laughed. "You're allowed to shoot an animal that's threatening you."

"So you felt pretty threatened?"

"That's my story and I'm sticking to it."

Garret chuckled. "So when's that romantic weekend going to happen?"

"This weekend. We decided against the room with the hot tub."

"Good idea. That would be funny if I didn't know the story behind it."

"I think it's funny. Pretty darned silly, actually. That doesn't mean I don't flip out when I get near a hot tub. But I think humor will help me get over it faster."

"It won't hurt."

"I'm *really* looking forward to this weekend. We're leaving the kids with Lois and Don. Christi and Terri will come over to help out. They thought it would be good practice. The Elk Horn has this separate wing for their bed and breakfast. I might leave the room to eat. But I wouldn't count on it. I plan to be busy."

"Good to see you acting like yourself again." Garret grinned. "You're the horniest reverend I've ever come across."

"You've probably never spent so much time with anyone like me."

"Very true. Maybe they're all that way."

"We're human. We love our wives and enjoy spending time alone with them. It's not something that happens often with three kids."

"And two more on the way."

Tony let his breath out. "Yeah."

"Sounds like you're having second thoughts."

"I've had second thoughts all along. This is a pretty big responsibility."

"Is everything going smoothly?"

"Yeah. We met with the grandmothers and uncle. The girls agreed that the ranch should be rented out for now. They'll decide next summer if they want to sell it. They both want to sell, because of the bad memories. But they may change their minds. Blake and Jill had a good insurance policy. That's going into a college fund. We'll get money from the state to cover their expenses till they graduate."

"And suddenly you're the parents of two teenaged girls." Garret shuddered with a grin. "I thanked God that we only had a boy when I heard other people talking about the horrors of raising girls."

Tony laughed. "I figure we're ahead of the game."

"How's that?"

"These girls are already in counseling, and probably will be for as long as they live with us. They'll have somewhere to talk about any problems that come up."

"Good point."

"Any news about me confronting Sue?"

"Not yet."

XXXV

Christi and Terri had time to settle into their room before supper. After everyone helped clear the table and Kelly started the dishwasher, she and Tony sat at the kitchen table with their two new charges.

"I guess we need to go over some rules," Tony said. "First, we don't intend to use you as free baby sitters. If we ask you to babysit, we'll pay you the going rate. You'll get an allowance every week. That's yours. You don't get it for doing chores. We all do chores because we're part of this family. We all contribute. If you need money for school supplies or fees, we'll take care of that."

"We have a car and a pickup," Christi said. "Can we get those?"

Tony made a face. "Yes. One. Later. Right now, I want to keep a pretty close eye on you. And you know why. I don't want you going anywhere alone. And you don't need a car to get around Spruce Lake. I believe in walking. We all walk unless we absolutely need the mini-van. It's better for us and saves money."

"He's the most frugal guy you're ever going to meet," Kelly said with a smile.

"Well," Christi offered. "We might as well have them both here right away. Couldn't you use a pickup once in a while?"

"Yes," Tony said. "I suppose. But I still wouldn't let you drive anywhere, unless Kelly or I were going with you."

"That's fine. I just want them here if any of us need them."

"Okay. We can do that. Now, I don't want either of you out after dark, unless somebody drives you. And I don't mean one of your friends. I'm talking about a parent."

"But ..." Terri said.

"Not open for debate. I'm just thinking of your safety. When they put

Caleb away, I won't be so overprotective."

Terri nodded. "Okay. I understand."

"And this is our house. We have a right to come into your room. But we'll try not to. We expect you to leave the door open when you're not in the room. So we also expect it to be clean. You'll find that we expect a lot of you."

"Tell me about it. I've never been any good at cleaning."

"You'll learn. We expect you to do your best in school. If you're having any problems, tell us. Kelly and I are pretty smart. And if we can't help you, we'll find someone who can. Any questions?"

"Are you, like, the strictest parents ever?"

Tony grinned. "I warned you."

***

"Kelly," Christi said, standing in the kitchen in her bathrobe. "I'm out of shampoo. Could I borrow some? I'll be late if I don't get moving."

Kelly glanced at her, then turned her attention back to feeding Justin, who had taken to throwing his food.

"Sure. It's in the bathroom. But Tony's taking a ... shower."

Christi had bolted down the hall. Kelly sat there staring while Christi opened the bathroom door.

"Hi, Tony. I need some shampoo. ... Thanks."

She left with a bottle in hand, closing the door behind her. Kelly continued to stare. In a moment, Tony came from the bathroom, wearing a towel, still wet, an amazed look on his face.

She regained her voice. "Tell me you were wearing that when she opened the door."

"Afraid not. I put this on after she left."

"I can't believe she did that."

"Oh, I can. She didn't see anything she hasn't seen before."

"Lock the door when you go in there."

"Good idea."

Terri shuffled into the kitchen, yawning. She poured her morning half cup of coffee and took it to the refrigerator for milk, before she noticed Tony. Her eyes widened. "Oh, my ... ! Christi was right. You do have a great body."

Tony moved behind a chair. "Well, this is getting more awkward by the minute."

"Just wait," Kelly said, trying not to smile. "It's about to get worse."

She nodded toward Christi, returning to the kitchen, her face bright red. "Did I just do that?"

Tony nodded. "I'll lock the door from now on."

"I'm so sorry. We expect you to respect our privacy and I do something like that."

"What'd you do?" Terri asked.

Christi ignored her. "I didn't think anything of it. Just Tony's body. Can I borrow some shampoo? I'm so embarrassed."

Tony shrugged. "No big deal. You sure woke me up."

"And he sure woke me up," Terri added.

Christi frowned. "Tony thinks it's no big deal. But, Kelly, what do you think?"

She smiled. "I think if he remembers to lock the bathroom door, you won't make that mistake again. And if he doesn't parade around in a towel, Terri will stop drooling on the floor. So I think this is all Tony's fault, don't you girls?"

"Hey," Tony said. "I don't think I like being outnumbered by women."

"Get used to it."

***

Garret met Tony and Kelly when they walked into the FBI's Denver Field Office. He regarded Tony's "deer in the headlights" expression.

"You going to be able to do this?"

Tony nodded. "I don't know what I'm going to say to her. But she'll get the message."

Kelly squeezed his hand and addressed Garret. "Are you sure I can't be in there with him?"

"It would be counterproductive. She might think he's just putting on a show to impress you. I'll be with him. You'll be able to watch through the glass."

"And you have a room where he can decompress afterward?"

"Right across the hall. I'll point it out on the way. You ready, Tony?"

He nodded. "Thanks for bringing her here from the jail. I'm pretty sure I couldn't have done this there."

"No problem. Let's go. I want you prepared when we go through the observation room. Her lawyer and her mother are there with the US Attorney."

"Okay. Thanks for the heads up."

But when he entered the room, Tony's eyes locked on Sue on the other side of the glass. She sat at a table in an orange prison jumpsuit, her cuffed hands in front of her. He walked to the glass, aware of conversation behind him, but not hearing the words.

He stared at her hands. "Take the cuffs off."

"Are you sure?" Garret asked.

Tony raised his right arm, revealing the scar still there. "They'll distract me."

Garret entered the room, removed the cuffs, then returned. Tony watched Sue rub her wrists for a moment longer. Without a word, he reached for the doorknob. Garret followed him inside.

When Sue saw Tony, her face lit up. "Tony! I knew you'd ..." Her smile faded. "Tony?"

He could not speak with his jaw clenched. He clamped his fists so tight that he began to shake. *I have to say something.* Forcing his mouth open failed to produce words. He closed it again.

Sue's eyes glistened and tears rolled down her cheeks.

Garret touched Tony's arm and he jerked away. He stood there shaking, feeling helpless again. *Why can't I say anything to her? I just want to hit her.*

He made an animal sound and slammed both fists on the table. She pushed back against her chair. He slammed his fists again and leaned as close to her as the table would allow. He just glared while her tears flowed.

Then he pivoted and swung the door open with a crash. He stalked through the other room opening the hallway door in a similar manner.

He finally noticed Kelly holding another door open for him. He bolted inside and paced around the conference room until he finally noticed her again. She talked, but he could not understand her words.

He focused on her lips as he approached. Then he pushed her against the wall in a passionate kiss.

Kelly overcame her shock and participated. *He needs to release his anger. This is better than throwing furniture.* She felt him become aroused and wished that she could have locked the door. *I wasn't expecting sex.*

But his passion cooled before he could go that far. He shoved himself away from her and walked to the table, leaning on it with both hands. He used a foot to pull out one of the wheeled chairs, sank into it, then leaned forward with his elbows on his legs.

Kelly rubbed his back. When he began shaking again, she stroked his hair. "I love you, Tony."

He sobbed. "I couldn't say anything. I blew the chance."

"You didn't have to. She got the message."

He leaned into her and Kelly held him while he cried.

***

More than an hour later, Kelly heard soft tapping on the door. She glanced at Tony, sleeping with his head on his arms on the table, before opening the door for Garret.

He looked around the room. "I thought I might have to buy new furniture."

"I thought we were going to have sex on the table."

Garret raised his thick eyebrows. "He's full of surprises."

"He didn't have quite that much energy left. Then he was upset because he couldn't say anything to her."

"Hellfire. They say a picture is worth a thousand words. An enraged victim in your face is worth a million. It only took about five minutes for her lawyer and her mother to get her to start talking. She gave us the location where they were supposed to meet and every other hideout they've ever used. I don't know what any of it's worth."

"He wouldn't have stayed there when nobody else showed up."

"That's what she said. When we asked her what he would have done under the circumstances, she confirmed what we had guessed. Caleb would change his appearance to fit in, then see what he could find out. It wouldn't take much effort for him to learn that Sue was captured and his father killed."

"So he'd go after Christi."

"She's carrying his child. He can't get to Sue. But he has some chance of getting to Christi. I asked if he might go to his mother for help. She said the siblings had discussed that as they got older. What they would do if anything happened to Jacob. They all agreed that their mother just didn't understand them. That's when Mrs. Brock left the room."

"That poor woman is another victim."

"The first one. You think you can wake him. He's going to get a backache sleeping like that. We can find him a better place to sleep."

"Let's see. He really exhausted himself."

It took quite a bit of shaking to rouse him. Tony sat up and rubbed his face. He noticed Garret. "I'm sorry. I blew it."

"Blew it? That was just the performance we needed. She spilled everything."

"She did? But I couldn't say anything."

"You didn't need to. You finally got it through her head that you weren't her man, you were her prisoner. Nothing we said could convince her of that."

"Oh. I don't feel any better."

"It's too soon for that. You need a couple days rest."

"Starting right now."

Kelly squeezed his shoulders. "You can sleep on the way home."

XXXVI

Tony rode Chance through the gold of the aspen leaves, never still, even on this calm fall day. He felt good, having returned to full duty, patrolling the park to offer assistance, the new Beretta on his belt. His old one had never been recovered.

After recuperating from his confrontation with Sue, his progress had accelerated. Releasing his rage had been cathartic. His attention span had improved. His interest in making love had increased until Kelly sometimes declined his invitation. He chuckled at that thought. These days, he felt good more often than not.

Twice, he stopped to talk to hikers. He looked for hazards, but for the most part, he could just enjoy the ride. Even though someone had ridden Chance regularly, they had not put on the miles that Tony did. The gelding had lost some condition. Tony pulled him up on Last Gasp Hill, a spot along the Boundary Ski and Hiking trail with a beautiful view of Spruce Lake.

He enjoyed the view, and the freedom. He once again felt comfortable in the park, no longer jumping at every shadow. Although Kelly and some of his friends felt differently. They probably would have kept him in town if he had not been wearing the vest.

He smiled and patted Chance's neck.

"Ready to get home?"

He held the gelding back as they descended the slope and even when they reached level ground. At this time of the afternoon, Chance not only knew that he was going home, he knew that his grain ration awaited him. Tony could count on having a handful of horse under those conditions.

But suddenly, Chance no longer pulled on his arm. Tony switched the reins from his right hand to his left. He casually rested the right on his Beretta, unsnapping the strap with his index finger. His muscles tightened, ready to leap from the saddle if he needed to. But he had entered a clearing with no cover. He kept his eyes on the thick stand of young aspen to which Chance's ears pointed.

Caleb stepped from cover, Tony's old Beretta in his hand. Tony pulled Chance to a stop. Caleb had shaved and cut his hair. He wore jeans, a plaid flannel shirt, and the Kevlar vest.

When the horse saw that what he had feared was only a man, he began to dance around the clearing, ready to go home again.

"Make him stand still," Caleb said.

"Caleb, you don't know much about horses. He wants to go home."

Tony nudged Chance with his left heel—the one Caleb could not see—while holding him back. Chance obediently side passed toward Caleb, who stepped out of the way.

"Drop your gun."

"I don't think so. I was a prisoner once. Didn't much like it."

Caleb scowled. Tony had guessed right. Caleb needed him alive to get to Christi. He did not want to kill Tony. Yet.

"Damn it, Tony. You stole my woman."

Chance's feet never stopped moving, though Tony controlled where he put them. Now he moved away from Caleb.

"She was never your woman. You dragged her from her home, killed her parents, and raped her. She was your prisoner."

"She's carrying my kid. You got no right to take my kid."

"You have no right to that kid. You raped her."

Chance had reached the edge of the small clearing, with a stand of dogwood bushes by his left side.

Tony leaped from the saddle, rolling in the air as he pulled his pistol. Caleb fired over Chance's back, but Tony had already fallen behind the horse.

Chance bolted toward home, forcing Caleb to jump out of his way and giving Tony time to find cover. Caleb fired twice into the dogwoods before Tony, ten yards to the left, returned fire. He aimed for Caleb's legs.

Caleb's knees buckled but he stayed on his feet. He backed, limping toward cover, firing at the spot where Tony had been.

This time Tony took his time, aiming higher. The shot spun Caleb around.

Tony rushed from cover and kicked the gun away from where Caleb had dropped it. He stood over his opponent, who lay groaning, grasping his wounded right arm.

Caleb grinned up at him. "Don't suppose you'd finish me off?"

"If I'd wanted to do that, it would be done."

Caleb nodded. "Didn't learn nothing from Seth. Just as dumb as he was. Let you catch me with no cover. Pa'd beat me if he was alive."

"Yeah."

"He was proud a you. Mad as hell, but proud. Said you just waited for your chance, then took it. And now you got the better a me. Took care a the whole family."

"You should have looked for wives the legal way."

"Guess so. Nobody bothered us till then. How's Sue?"

"In jail."

"And her baby?"

"There was no baby."

"Huh. She was pretty sure a it."

"She was wrong."

"But Christi's having my kid, right?"

"Yeah. But you're going to jail for life."

"Doesn't matter. The family will go on, even if the name don't."

Tony heard the sound of the park's all terrain vehicles and realized that the shooting had been heard from park headquarters. He tried his radio.

"Evergreen one this is Evergreen five."

Kelly's voice came on, shrill. "Tony!"

"I'm fine. But Caleb needs an ambulance."

This time Don's voice replied. "You sure you're okay?"

"I probably have some scrapes and bruises. Did Chance make it back there yet?"

"Ran in the barn when Red and Tim were leaving. They there yet?"

"Just about."

"They got first aid kits. I called Ryan and Garret. When they get here, I'll tell them you got things under control. I'll call the ambulance eventually."

"We should be able to stop the bleeding when they get here. He'll survive till he can get to a hospital."

"Too bad. Where'd you shoot him?"

"The arm and leg."

Don growled. "I was hoping for somewhere a little more private."

Tony chuckled into his radio as Red and Tim pulled up. They had heard enough of his conversation to know not to expect a fire fight.

"I'll talk to you in a while, Don." He directed his co-workers. "Leave your guns and knives there. Bring the first aid kits and patch him up. We don't want him bleeding to death before Garret gets here." He pulled out his handcuffs. "Caleb, give me your hands."

Tony holstered his gun and cuffed Caleb's hands before turning him over to Red and Tim.

"You okay?" Red asked Tony.

"Yeah. I'm great, really."

"Guess we didn't need to worry about you."

Caleb laughed. "Worry? Bout him? Thought I knew what to expect from him. Had my gun ready and he still got the drop on me. Nobody needs to worry bout him."

***

"I'm going to miss you," Tony said.

Garret laughed. "I'll miss this place. I don't think I've ever spent six months in one place since I started working for the bureau."

"I thought you'd lived in the same place since I've known you."

"I'm never there. This is the first time I've stayed in one place so long that my wife came looking for me. And she's fallen in love with Spruce Lake. She stopped by the real estate office yesterday."

Tony grinned. "Did she get sticker shock?"

"Prices are a little high. But we can sell our house for a whole lot more. If we find the right place, I'll go along with the move. I can keep an apartment in Denver. I like the idea of living where I can hunt and fish."

"Wouldn't mind having you around. Like you say, you're never home enough to get to be a pain in the neck."

"Well, somebody has to keep you out of trouble."

"*Keep* me out of trouble. You're the one who *gets* me into trouble."

"One time. You're never going to let me live that down, are you?"

Tony laughed. "Not a chance."

###

Made in the USA
Columbia, SC
06 May 2025

57592399R00122